The Valley of the Lost

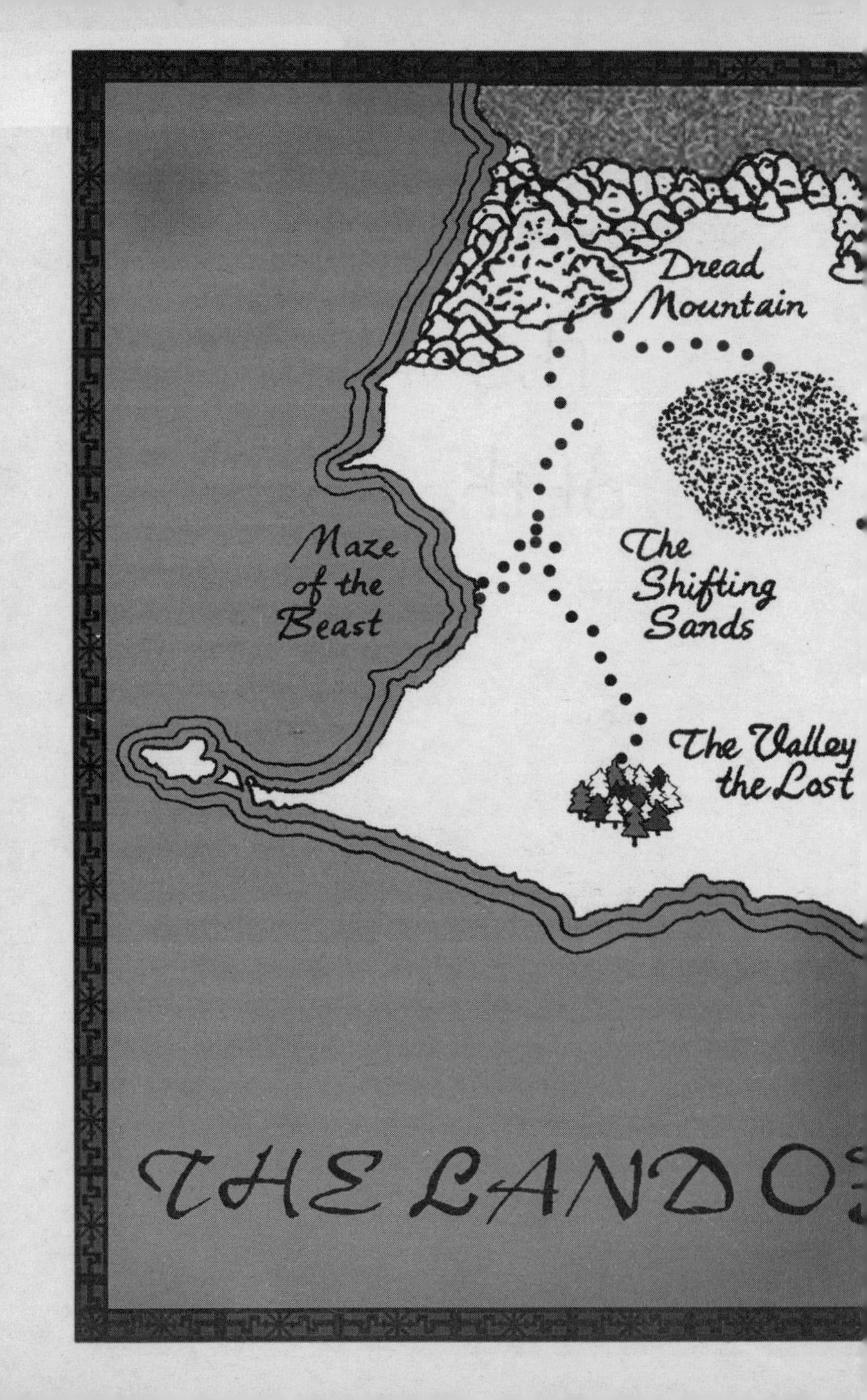
Dread Mountain
Maze of the Beast
The Shifting Sands
The Valley
the Lost
THE LAND O

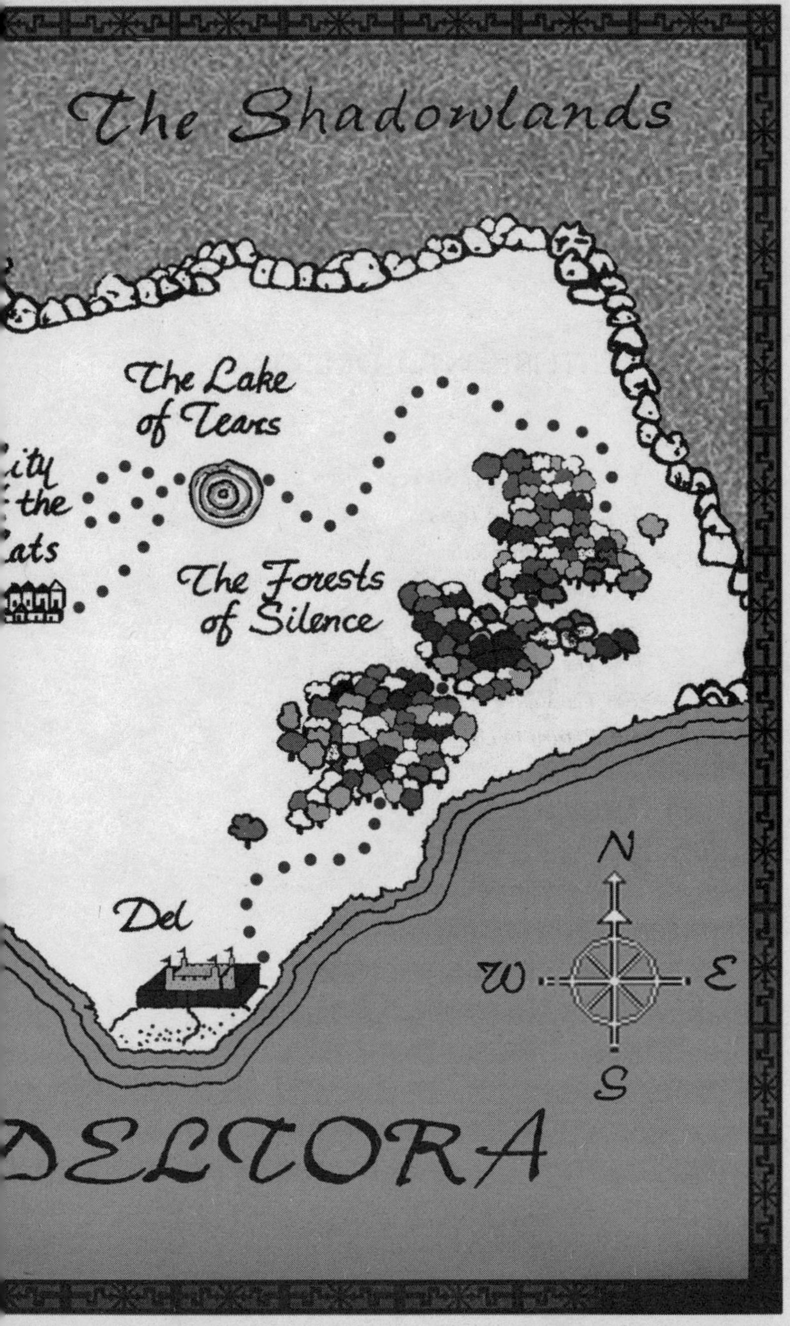

The Shadowlands

The Lake of Tears

The Forests of Silence

Del

N

W

E

S

DELTORA

VENTURE INTO DELTORA

1 ❋ *The Forests of Silence*

2 ❋ *The Lake of Tears*

3 ❋ *City of the Rats*

4 ❋ *The Shifting Sands*

5 ❋ *Dread Mountain*

6 ❋ *The Maze of the Beast*

7 ❋ *The Valley of the Lost*

8 ❋ *Return to Del*

The Valley of the Lost

EMILY RODDA

Scholastic Inc.
New York Toronto London Auckland Sydney
Mexico City New Delhi Hong Kong Buenos Aires

ISBN 0-439-25329-2

12 11 10 9 8 3 4 5 6/0
40

Printed in the U.S.A.
First American edition, October 2001

Contents

The story so far...

Lief, Barda, and Jasmine are on a great quest to find the seven lost gems of the magic Belt of Deltora. Hidden in fearsome places throughout the land, the gems must be restored to the Belt before the rightful heir to the throne can be found and the evil Shadow Lord's tyranny ended.

Six gems have been found so far. The topaz, symbol of faith, has the power to contact the spirit world and to clear the mind. The ruby, for happiness, pales when danger threatens, repels evil spirits, and is an antidote to venom. The opal, gem of hope, gives glimpses of the future. The lapis lazuli, the heavenly stone, is a powerful talisman. The emerald, for honor, dulls in the presence of evil. The amethyst, for truth, calms and soothes.

The companions have discovered a secret resistance movement led by the mysterious Doom. Another member of the Resistance, Dain, a young man of about Lief's own age, has been kidnapped by pirates, and Lief's parents have been imprisoned.

In constant fear of the Shadow Lord's Grey Guards and hideous shape-changing Ols, the companions must now cross the River Tor and journey to their last goal, the Valley of the Lost, where the last stone lies, the great diamond.

Now read on . . .

1 - Night Terrors

It was dark and very still. Lief, Barda, and Jasmine slipped through the night like shadows, and the River Tor slid beside them, keeping its secrets.

They had decided that for safety's sake they should not travel by day. But the night held its own perils, for they did not dare to use a torch to light their way, and the moon was shrouded in cloud. As the darkness cloaked them, so also would it cloak a prowling enemy.

And it hid more than that. It hid holes, rocks, and ditches. It hid trees, bushes, and landmarks. Every step was a step into the unknown.

They knew that somewhere ahead there was a bridge. When they reached it they could at last cross the river that had caused them so much grief. Then they could begin moving towards the Valley of the Lost, where lay the great diamond, the seventh gem of the Belt of Deltora.

But in this blackness how easy it would be to pass the bridge unaware! So, though all of them loathed the very thought of the River Tor, they stayed close beside it, knowing that its dark waters must lead them to their goal at last.

With one hand Lief gripped the Belt of Deltora, hidden under his clothes. But the Belt, for all its power, could not help him as his eyes strained to penetrate the darkness ahead.

"It is not far now," Jasmine whispered suddenly.

Lief saw a faint, pale blur as her face turned to him. Filli, curled inside her jacket, made a small, sleepy sound. Kree was silent and invisible on her shoulder, his black feathers swallowed by the darkness.

"Do you see it?" asked Barda.

"No," Jasmine breathed. "But I smell people and animals, and the bridge was just beyond a village, remember?"

They crept forward, and at last found themselves moving through cleared ground. Lief thought he could make out the thicker blackness of a wall rising to his left.

Perhaps armed villagers on night watch stood behind the wall, listening for danger. Perhaps this was why the village still stood, despite the pirates that sailed the Tor's waters and the bandits that prowled its banks.

If they heard a sound, the guards would investigate. They would strike instantly, without pity. They would have learned from sad examples all along the river that to hesitate was to risk losing everything.

The companions moved on, treading lightly, scarcely breathing. No sooner had they reached the safety of a grove of trees beyond the wall, when the clouds covering the moon parted and the ground was flooded with light.

Jasmine caught her breath. "We were fortunate," she murmured. "If that had happened just a moment earlier . . ."

Barda nudged Lief's arm and pointed ahead. Through the trees Lief saw the bridge. It was very close, peaceful in the moonlight. A small herd of long-haired goats clustered around it, some standing, some resting on the grass.

The bridge was solid and broad enough to take a cart. A large sign stood beside it. The sign's lettering was faded, but Lief could still make out the words.

Lief's heart thumped. Tora! The great city of the west, so loyal to the kings and queens of Deltora. The ideal hiding place for the heir to the throne.

Tora must be near. But there had been no sign of a city as they followed the river down to the coast just days ago. At the time, Lief had thought little of it. He had too many other things to worry about. Now, however, it seemed very strange indeed. For surely Tora was set on the River Tor. Its very name made a link.

"Tora must be set well back from the river," muttered Barda, whose thoughts had plainly been running on the same lines. "But it is odd that we did not see it in the distance, at least."

Lief nodded, still puzzling over the mystery. "Perhaps we passed it at night, and it keeps no lights. In any case, we may yet be able to visit it — on our way to the Valley of the Lost."

"By all reports, we would be advised not to do any such thing, at least until the Belt is complete," hissed Jasmine. "Dain was warned — "

She broke off, biting her lip, and Lief and Barda were also silent. Memories of the boy they had last seen bound and helpless in the pirates' coastal cave flooded all their minds.

Dain had longed to go to Tora. Now he would never see it. Even now the pirates were sailing up the river with him. In a few days he would be handed over to the Grey Guards. Though Lief, Barda, and Jasmine knew they could not save him, his sad and frightened eyes haunted them all.

The boy would try his best to escape. But what hope did he have against a gang of armed ruffians greedy for the Shadow Lord's gold?

Jasmine tossed her head as if to shake away unwelcome thoughts, and turned her attention to the goats by the bridge. "We will have to move slowly, so as not to startle the beasts," she said. "If they make a sound, all is lost."

"They must be used to people." Lief stared at the goats, at the small horns gleaming, the long, smooth hair. "But we should show ourselves to them now, while the moon shines. We will frighten them if we come at them in the dark."

He took a single step forward, then stopped abruptly, his eyes widening. One of the goats — there was something wrong with one of the goats! Its body seemed to be rippling, billowing outward like a ballooning sail.

Lief blinked rapidly. What trick of the moonlight

was this? Now that he looked again, the goat was exactly as before. Yet — he felt Barda grip his arm, saw another of the goats quiver and alter, head stretching upward, body shuddering, before returning to its normal shape. Then he knew. He had just seen what Dain had called the Tremor.

"Ols!" he breathed. "They are not goats at all, but Ols!" His stomach turned over as he realized how nearly they had walked into the midst of the herd, all unsuspecting. How nearly they had met their deaths.

"They are guarding the bridge." Barda gritted his teeth in frustration. "What will we do?"

"One of us must lead them away, so that the other two can slip across," said Jasmine. "I will — "

Barda shook his head firmly. "There are far too many of them for that trick to work, Jasmine. Some will give chase, some will stay. And now I come to think of it, there were many water birds roosting on the other side of the bridge when I passed it on my way to the coast. More Ols, no doubt, though I did not realize it at the time. And surely they will be there still."

"Then we must go on," muttered Lief. "Move around the bridge, so that the Ols do not see us. Find another way across the river, farther upstream."

"But there *is* no other way!" hissed Jasmine. "I cannot swim, you know that. And even if I could, the killer worms — "

"We cannot swim, but there are such things as

boats," Barda broke in calmly. "We have money to pay for a crossing. Or we will make a raft. Anything would be better than fighting twenty Ols."

As silently as they had come, they crept away from the river and continued upstream, making a wide arc around the bridge. Now and then, through gaps in the trees, they caught glimpses of the goats still waiting, unmoving, in the moonlight.

*

When dawn broke, the sun struggling to shine through a blanket of cloud, the village and the bridge were far behind them. They stopped to eat and rest, huddling together beneath a group of ragged bushes. Kree took flight, to catch insects and stretch his cramped wings.

Lief had first watch. He wrapped his cloak around him and tried to make himself comfortable. His eyes were prickling, but he was not afraid that he would fall asleep. His body was jumping with nerves.

Time crawled by. Kree returned, and went to roost low in one of the bushes. Sulky dawn gave way to dull morning. Clouds hung low above Lief's head, thickening by the moment. We will have rain, he thought dismally. Scuttling animals had made narrow paths through the greenery, but there were no animals to be seen now, and for this Lief was grateful. Every living thing was suspect, in a place where Ols prowled.

And Doom claimed that there were Ols who

could take the form of things that were not living — Grade 3 Ols, the perfection of the Shadow Lord's evil art. If the tale was true, and such beings really existed, the very bush on which Kree perched, or the pebble at Lief's feet, could be a secret enemy. At any moment a horrible transformation could begin. At any moment a white, flickering specter with the Shadow Lord's mark in its core could rise and overwhelm them.

Nowhere was safe. Nothing could be trusted.

Lief licked his lips, fought down the dread that clutched his heart. But still his flesh seemed to tremble on his bones. He slipped his hands under his shirt and felt for the Belt of Deltora, heavy at his waist. His fingers moved to the sixth stone, the amethyst. As they rested upon it, as its magic flowed through him, the trembling slowly ebbed.

Somehow we will find a boat, he told himself. We will cross the river. Our quest will continue. We will survive.

But still he could not rid himself of the feeling that they were caught in a net. A net that the Shadow Lord was slowly, slowly drawing in.

2 - Company

Late in the morning Barda woke and Lief took his turn to sleep. He opened his eyes in mid-afternoon to find the sky leaden and the earth breathless. His head ached dully as he sat up. His sleep had been heavy, his dreams confused and disturbing.

Barda and Jasmine were strapping up their packs.

"We think we should move on, Lief, as soon as you are ready," said Barda. "It is almost as dark as night as it is, and if we wait for true darkness we will cover little distance before the rain sets in."

"The other village we saw on our way down to the coast cannot be far away," Jasmine added, turning away to peer through the bushes to the land beyond. "If we reach it before nightfall we may be able to persuade someone to row us across the river."

Lief felt a spurt of anger. They had been talking while he slept, making plans without him. No doubt they had been impatiently waiting for him to wake, thinking he was a sleepyhead. Did they not know how tired he was? He had slept for hours, yet he was still very weary — so weary that he felt a week of sleep would not satisfy him.

Almost at once, he realized that his annoyance was a result of that very tiredness. He looked at Jasmine's heavy eyes, and the deep, grey lines on Barda's face. They were as exhausted as he was. He forced a smile, nodded, and began pulling together his own belongings.

*

By the time they reached the next village, it was even darker, but night had not yet fallen. The companions moved cautiously through the open gate in the wall.

The place was a ruin. Everything not made of stone had been burned to cinders. The familiar names "Finn," "Nak," and "Milne" were scrawled on the walls left standing.

"They wrote their names here in triumph, thinking they were kings instead of thieving, murderous pirates," Jasmine muttered savagely. "I am glad they died screaming."

"And I," said Barda, with feeling.

Lief wanted to agree. Once, it would have been easy for him to do so. But thinking of how Milne, especially, had met his terrible fate, gibbering with terror in the Maze of the Beast, somehow he could not. Revenge did not seem sweet to him any longer. There had been too much suffering.

He turned away, and began searching the ruins. But there was nothing to find. There were no people, no animals left in this dead place. There was no shelter.

And there was no boat.

With heavy hearts, Lief, Barda, and Jasmine moved slowly on.

*

The rain began at midnight. At first it pelted down, stinging their hands and faces. Then it settled into a steady stream that soaked them through and chilled them to the bone. Kree hunched miserably on Jasmine's shoulder. Filli, bedraggled, hid his head inside her jacket.

They plodded through mud and darkness, trying to keep alert, watching for anything that would help them cross the river. But there were no trees — only low bushes. There were no logs or planks washed up on the shore. Nothing they passed could be used to make a raft.

At dawn they rested fitfully, finding what shelter they could under dripping leaves. But after a few hours the ground on which they lay began to run with water. They staggered up, and began to tramp again.

And so the time went on. By the beginning of the third night of rain, they had stopped looking for a way across the river, now swollen and overflowing its banks. The rain screened their view of the other side, even by day, but Lief and Barda knew that by now they must be opposite the great reed beds that had stopped their progress on the way downstream. It would be no use crossing here, even if they could find something to carry them. They knew, from bitter experience, what it was like to flounder through that oozing mud.

"Is this fiendish river forever to bar our way?" Jasmine groaned, as they stopped to rest once more. "And will this rain never stop?"

"If we can keep going a little longer, we will be opposite the place where Broad River joins the Tor," Barda said. "I know that there are trees there, at least. We can make a shelter, and rest until the rain stops. We might even keep a fire going."

On they walked, in a dream of wet, cold darkness. Then, after what seemed a very long time, Jasmine abruptly stopped.

"What is it?" Lief whispered.

Jasmine's wet hand clutched his sleeve. "Sshh! Listen!"

Lief frowned, trying to concentrate. At first, all he could hear was the pounding of the rain and the rushing of the swollen river. Then voices came to him. Rough, angry voices. Shouting.

The companions moved slowly forward. Then,

not far ahead, they saw a winking light. They had not seen it before because it was masked by trees.

Trees! Lief realized that they had at last reached the shelter they had been seeking. But others had reached it before them. The light was a lantern hung from a branch. It flickered as dark figures moved around it, blocking it now and again from view.

The voices grew louder.

"I tell you, we must go back!" a man roared. "The more I think of it, the more I am sure. We should not have agreed to leave Nak and Finn alone with the booty. How do we know they will still be there when we return?"

Lief shook his head. Was he imagining things? Had he heard the man say "Nak" and "Finn"? Could the figures in the grove of trees be the pirates who had set sail to take Dain up the river to the Grey Guards? But what were they doing here? He had thought they would be far upstream by now.

"Nak and Finn will be waiting for us, all right, Gren," growled another of the pirates. "Whatever they say, they will want their share of the gold we get for that puny Resistance wretch on the ship."

They were talking about Dain! Lief strained to see beyond the trees to the river, and thought he caught a glimpse of the pale, furled sails of the pirate boat. The boat must be at anchor quite near to the shore. And Dain was on it!

"You are a trusting fool, Rabin!" shouted the man called Gren. "If I am right, Nak and Finn have more than a handful of gold to think about! Why else would they have let us come upriver alone? Do you really believe they are afraid of this man Doom? What is he but a Resistance wretch like the other?"

"They must have stopped when the rain set in," whispered Barda. "Perhaps the river began running too swiftly for them to move against the current. They came ashore, for shelter."

"Then a rowing boat must be here, on the river-bank," Jasmine breathed.

"Nak and Finn would not betray us!" a woman shrieked angrily. "You are a traitor yourself to say it, Gren. Beware! Remember what happened to Milne."

Other voices murmured angrily.

"Do not threaten me, you hag!" snarled the man. "Where is your own memory? Do you not remember one of the prisoners in the cavern telling us that Finn had secretly found a great gem? What if it is true?"

"A gem found in the Maze of the Beast?" jeered Rabin. "Oh, yes, that is very likely, I am sure! Are you weak in the head, Gren, that you could believe such fairy tales?"

"Shut your ugly mouth, Rabin!" Gren's voice was thick with rage.

"Shut your own, you fat fool!"

There was a roar, a sudden, violent movement, and a groan of agony.

"Oh, you devil!" screamed the woman.

Something crashed against the lantern. The light swung wildly and went out.

"Keep off!" Gren roared. "Why, you — "

"Take your hands off her!" several other voices shouted furiously.

Then, suddenly, the grove seemed to explode with sound as the rest of the crew joined the fight. Over the beating of the rain rose shouts and grunts, the clashing of steel, the breaking of branches, thumps and shrieks.

"To the river!" Barda muttered. "Quickly!"

3 - Adrift

The boat, filled ankle-deep with rainwater, was bobbing at the river's edge. No doubt it had been pulled onto dry land when the last of the pirates came ashore. But the river had risen since, and set it afloat. If it had not been tied to a tree, it would have drifted away.

It took a matter of moments for Barda to untie the rope while his companions crawled into the boat, Kree fluttering after them. By the time the big man clambered to the oars, they were already beginning to move into deeper water.

Shouts and screams from the trees still pierced the drumming of the rain. Not far away, the pirate ship strained at anchor. Two portholes in its side glowed like eyes. Lief had not noticed that before. Frantically scooping water from the bottom of the boat, he peered at the ship's deck, looking for a sign of movement.

Meanwhile, Barda was struggling with the oars. But he was not expert at the task, and the swollen waters of the river surged around the boat, fighting his every movement, pushing them downstream.

"The current is too strong for me! I do not know if I can get to the ship," he roared, shaking his wet hair from his brow.

"You must!" Jasmine cried. And only then did Lief realize how desperately she wanted Dain to be saved. She had said nothing before, appearing to accept the boy's loss with the calm she always showed in the face of disaster. But now that Dain was so near, she could not face the thought of leaving him behind.

Gritting his teeth, Lief threw down the pail and crawled to the rower's bench. "Make way!" he shouted, and squeezed himself down beside Barda, seizing an oar. He had never rowed before, but he had seen the pirates do it only days ago. He thought he could copy what they had done. Together he and Barda bent forward, pulled back, bent and pulled again.

The extra weight upon the oars began to take effect. Slowly, painfully, the boat drew nearer to the pirate ship. Then there was a shout. A shout, not from the shore, but from the ship itself.

Lief glanced around. A figure was standing on

the deck, waving frantically. It was Dain. A smaller figure capered by his side, a lantern swinging wildly in its hand. Lief realized that it was the odd little thieving creature Dain had called a polypan. The pirates must have left it onboard with Dain. And somehow he had persuaded it to set him free.

Dain had lifted a coil of rope attached by one end to the boat's deck. He began swinging it, as if he was about to throw.

"Here!" exclaimed Jasmine. She staggered to her feet, holding out her hands. The boat rocked dangerously.

"Sit down!" roared Barda. "You will have us over! Lief, row!"

Then Jasmine gave a cry, Kree screeched, and the boat jerked and rolled. Lief glanced again over his shoulder. The dark shape of the pirate ship, its glowing porthole eyes staring, loomed very near.

Dain had thrown the rope, and Jasmine had caught it. The slender line stretched tightly between the two rocking craft. It seemed that surely it must snap, but though it creaked and thinned, it did not break.

"I cannot hold it!" Jasmine shouted. Already she was leaning perilously over the bow, water foaming just below her head. Filli was chattering with fear on her shoulder, unable to help, terrified of falling. Kree fluttered beside them, screeching in panic.

Barda dropped his oar and scrambled towards

them. He took the weight of the rope in his own powerful hands and heaved. The boat lurched and wallowed in the swell. Lief grasped both oars and did his best to fight the current alone.

"Go back, Dain!" he heard Barda shout. "We will come aboard!" Again Lief risked turning to look. Dain, with the polypan close behind him, was climbing frantically down a rope ladder that hung from the ship's side directly between the shining porthole eyes. The polypan still held the lantern. It looked like a third eye, an eye that flickered and swung.

But — Lief squinted through the rain — the other two eyes were flickering as well. And surely they were brighter, far brighter, than they had been before.

"Dain!" Barda roared furiously. "Dain! This boat is too small. We cannot — "

Dain must have heard, but took no notice. He turned and made ready to jump, clinging to the ladder with one hand. His hair was streaming with water, plastered to his head. His face, gleaming in the lamplight, was desperate. Above him the polypan gibbered and swung, shaking the ladder in panic.

Then Lief smelled smoke, and understood.

"Fire!" he shouted.

As the word left his mouth there was a roar from somewhere in the ship's belly. The portholes shattered and jets of flame belched from them. Great cracks opened in the ship's side, and the gaps were filled with raging fire. The rain hissed and steamed as it hit the burning wood.

Dain and the polypan leaped together, crashing down into the rowboat. It tilted sideways, a great wave of water surging over the side, throwing Lief backwards, tearing the oars from his hands.

The boat righted itself again. It wallowed in the swell, rapidly drifting sideways, weighed down by two extra passengers and the water that swirled inside it. Stunned by his fall, Dain lay slumped against a seat as Jasmine bailed frantically and Lief and Barda scrambled for the oars. The polypan screamed, clinging to the point of the bow. It knew boats. It knew all too well what could happen to this one.

Cries of rage rose from the riverbank. The pirates had heard the noise, discovered the loss of the boat and seen the fire. Lief, grimly trying to keep the boat steady, saw their shadows leaping in the glow of the lantern they had lit once more. But that tiny glow was nothing compared to the inferno that the ship had become.

It seemed incredible that fire could rage while rain poured from above and angry water rushed below. But the fire had started below the deck, and roared out of control through the stores.

"It was the polypan!" Dain shouted, pulling himself upright. "It threw a lantern into the cabin under the deck where the oil, grease, and paint are stored. The rain and the pirates' beatings have driven it mad!"

As has its longing for the brown gum it loves to chew, perhaps, thought Lief, staring at the screeching, long-armed figure clinging to the bow. Ah, how it must wish it had never left the *River Queen*.

"We must get away from the ship!" Barda roared over the rain. "If it begins to sink it will pull us down with it!"

He and Lief bent again to the oars. But their clumsy efforts were of little use. Nothing seemed to stop that perilous sideways drift. As fast as Jasmine bailed, more water splashed over the side.

The polypan shrieked, its eyes glazed with terror. Then, without any warning, it suddenly sprang from its place at the bow and leaped for Lief and Barda, thrusting them aside and seizing the oars itself.

Cursing, Barda lunged for it.

"No!" shouted Lief. "Leave it! It can row far better than we can. It can save us all!"

With two deft sweeps of the oars, the polypan turned the boat. Then, back bending, powerful arms bulging, it began to row. And as if the boat recognized that at last it was in the hands of an expert, it began to cut through the swell like a knife through warm butter. In moments it had pulled clear of the burning ship and was heading straight across the river.

Jasmine continued to bail and as the water

slowly disappeared from the bottom of the boat their speed increased. Soon the burning ship was far behind them. They knew that ahead was the broad, straight water of Broad River, and the bridge that arched over it. Ahead, too, was the sad village of Where Waters Meet, and the little jetty that bore the *River Queen* sign.

Filli chattered excitedly, snuffling the air.

"We are very close!" Jasmine exclaimed. "We are almost at the bank!"

The polypan turned, baring its brown, chattering teeth. Its arms did not stop their work for a moment, but its eyes seemed to burn as they searched the darkness.

Water swirled around them as the swollen waters of the two rivers mingled. The boat raced forward. It is like cutting through a whirlpool, Lief thought, gripping his seat. If the polypan was not rowing, we would never survive this.

But the next moment, the polypan was not rowing. It had jumped from its place, abandoning the oars. It was springing to the bow and leaping past Jasmine and Dain — out and away into the darkness.

There was a thump, and the sound of running feet.

"The jetty!" Jasmine screamed.

Wildly she leaned from the boat, snatching at the piers of the old jetty, at the pole that supported the *River Queen* sign. But the raging water snatched the boat away before she could take hold. Then the boat was being swept down the river, spinning, spinning. One of the dragging oars dug deep into the water, pulled free, toppled into the swirling tide and was lost.

Barda lunged for the other, but reached it too late. Before he could grasp it, it had followed its fellow.

Then the companions could do nothing — nothing but cling to the sides of their lurching craft, as the treacherous waters swept them away.

4 - Silence

Stillness. Silence. Pink light through closed eyelids. Lief woke in confusion. Lay still in fear. The last thing he remembered was the boat crashing against something, spinning around, then continuing its mad, swirling dash into darkness.

Did I fall asleep? he thought. How could that be?

But he *had* slept, or else fainted. That much was clear. For here he was, waking. The rain had stopped. The terrible night had passed.

Or — was this death? This light, peaceful drifting — was it how all the struggle ended?

He opened his eyes. The sky was pink above him. Dawn.

Slowly he sat up. Before him was a lake — a huge lake, smooth as glass. Jasmine slept beside him, her cheek on the hard boards of a bench, Kree standing guard beside her. Barda lay not far away, breathing steadily. And Dain — Dain was sitting in the bow, his dark eyes filled with wonder.

Lief wet his lips. "Where are we?" he heard himself ask huskily. "What happened?"

"We hit something — a sandbar, I think, made by the flood," Dain said slowly. "It must have knocked us into a channel separated from the main river. So we floated here, into the great lake, instead of being swept farther downstream."

"But there is no lake beside the River Tor!" Lief protested. He shook his head, unable to believe his own eyes. Yet he could see in the distance the broad band of the river moving on to the sea.

"Once, it seems, there was a lake," said Dain softly. "And now, because of the flood, there is a lake again. Do you not see? These are the reed beds, Lief. Now they are a lake, as once they always were. And now there is no fog to hide what lies at the lake's edge."

He pointed. Lief turned. And there, directly behind him, was dry land and a vast shimmer of light.

"It is Tora," Dain whispered. "Tora."

Lief narrowed his eyes against the dazzling glare, and finally made out the gleaming shapes of towers, turrets, and walls. In his amazement he thought at first that the buildings themselves were shining, glowing from within by some sort of magic.

Then he realized that the shimmer was caused by the rays of the early morning sun striking thousands of hard white surfaces, polished smooth.

He looked away, rubbing his streaming eyes. It was impossible to see the city clearly. And yet, he had seen enough to feel puzzled, as well as filled with awe, at its silent, untouched beauty.

"Tora was carved by magic from a marble mountain," said Dain. "It is perfect — all of one piece, without crack or seam."

His voice seemed stronger, deeper. Lief glanced at him, wondering, and saw that he was sitting very upright. As had happened once before since Lief had known him, he suddenly looked older, prouder, and less frail. His mouth was firm. His eyes were shining. It was as though a mask had dropped from his face, leaving it unguarded.

He felt Lief's gaze and turned away quickly. "Now would be a good time to enter the city," he said, in his normal voice. "It is very early. Most people will not yet be stirring."

Without waiting for an answer, he crept gently to the end of the boat, and climbed onto the shore. The boat rocked gently. Jasmine and Barda opened their eyes and sat up, startled.

"It — it is all right," Lief stammered. "We are safe. The flood has refilled an old lake. And it seems — it seems we have reached Tora."

As Dain had done, he pointed. And as he himself

had done only moments before, Barda and Jasmine turned and blinked into the shimmering light.

"So Tora was on the river after all!" Jasmine exclaimed. "Or, at least, on a lake beside the river."

"And does Dain think we can walk calmly into the place without being stopped?" muttered Barda. "Tora is controlled by the enemy."

Lief frowned. "That is what Doom said. But — I am starting to wonder if he was telling the truth. I cannot see the city clearly, but there seem to be no Grey Guards at the gate. No mark of the Shadow Lord on the walls. No damage or destruction or rubbish lying about. And it is so peaceful, Barda. Have you ever known a place overrun by Guards to be so?"

Barda hesitated. Then he rubbed his hand across his dry mouth. "Is it possible?" he whispered. "Can it be that the Torans' magic has been strong enough to repel even the Shadow Lord's evil? If so, Lief . . . if so . . ."

Lief's heart was thudding with excitement. "If so, the heir to Deltora may be there. Waiting for us."

The city lay before them, silent, waiting, cloaked in light. The shore of the lake stretched empty and inviting before them. Yet the moment Lief set foot upon it, his excitement vanished, and he was gripped by fear.

Head bent, he slowly followed Dain, struggling with the fear, trying to understand it. Was it a natural caution, a reluctance to plunge half blinded into a place where, despite appearances, enemies might lurk? Was it fear of the powerful magic of Tora itself?

Or was it because, now that the moment had almost certainly come, he feared to meet the heir of Deltora?

He raised his head and with a shock saw that Dain was almost at the edge of the shore. The lonely figure hesitated for a split second, then stepped forward into dazzling light and disappeared. Lief squinted and rubbed his eyes as again they began to water, blurring his view.

He stumbled forward, pulling his cloak around him to hide his sword. We must not look like enemies, he thought confusedly. We must . . .

"Lief!" he heard Barda call sharply, and realized that his companions had lost sight of him. Every thread of his cloak was glittering, surrounding him with light. He answered the call and waited. Barda and Jasmine reached him in moments, their arms held over their dazzled eyes.

Together they walked the last few steps to the city's walls. Gradually they became one with the light, and it no longer blinded them. They reached the shore's end. Tora rose before them in all its vast splendor.

Tora was carved by magic from a marble mountain. It is all of one piece — perfect, without crack or seam.

They stopped for a moment, awestruck. Then,

their hands held out in front of them to show they meant no harm, they moved through the vast white archway that was the city's entrance.

At once they were swept by a tingling chill. It was like being plunged into a deep bath of cool, clear water. For a moment, time seemed to stand still, and Lief lost all sense of where he was or what he was supposed to be doing. When he came to himself he realized that his dazzled eyes had deceived him. He had thought that the arch was merely a gateway, but it was much thicker than he had thought. Instead of moving straight into the city, he and his companions were standing in the shade of an echoing tunnel. Smooth whiteness curved around them.

Kree crooned and clucked, swaying slightly on Jasmine's arm.

"What was that?" Jasmine whispered. "That — feeling?"

Lief shook his head uncertainly. But he was not afraid. In fact, he felt more at peace than he ever remembered being in his life.

Slowly they walked to the end of the tunnel, and emerged at last into the city light.

No robed figures waited to greet them. No Grey Guards jumped, sneering, into their way. The silence was eerie. Their boots echoed on the broad, gleaming street.

Turning to one side, Lief pulled up his shirt and

looked at the Belt of Deltora. The ruby glowed as brightly as ever. So they were not in danger yet. But — the emerald!

Lief stared. The emerald had lost all color. It had become as dull and lifeless as it had been when it was possessed by the monster Gellick on Dread Mountain. What did that mean? Was evil here? Or . . . he seemed to remember that something else could dull the emerald. What was it?

He and his companions paced on. Halls and houses, towers and palaces, rose, shining, on either side of them. Through tall windows and open doors, rich hangings, silken rugs, and fine furniture could be seen. Everywhere flowers in window boxes bloomed, bright and humming with bees. Fruit trees thrived in huge pots, clustered around courtyards where tables of food and drink stood ready and fountains splashed.

But no one sat by the fountains, tended the trees, or ate the food. No one walked along the streets, or peered from the windows of the houses. No one stood on the silken rugs, or rested in the fine chairs. The city was utterly deserted.

"It is like Where Waters Meet," whispered Jasmine.

"No," Barda said grimly. "Where Waters Meet was in ruins. But here — why, it looks as though the people left it only five minutes ago."

He looked over his shoulder. "How powerful is

the Torans' magic?" he muttered. "Could it be that they have made themselves invisible? And where is Dain?"

Wondering, the hair on the backs of their necks prickling, they moved on through the empty marble streets.

At last, they reached a huge square at the city's heart, and there at least one of Barda's questions was answered, for there they found Dain.

Great halls decorated with tall columns surrounded the square. The largest of these stood at the top of a sweeping flight of broad steps. A carved box lay on the top step. It looked out of place — as though it had been brought there for a purpose and then abandoned.

But Dain had not climbed the steps. He was crouched at the foot of a huge piece of marble that rose in the square's center. Lief knew at once that it was the stone his father had described seeing in the painting at the palace in Del. But no green flames flickered from the stone's peak. And it was cracked through.

Dain did not move as Lief, Barda, and Jasmine strode towards him. Even when they reached him and spoke his name he did not seem to notice they were there. His eyes, dull and hopeless, were fixed on the stone.

Words were carved on the marble. The jagged crack ran through them like a wound:

We, the people of Tora, swear loyalty to Adin,
King of Deltora, and all of his blood who follow him.
If ever this vow is broken, may this rock,
our city's heart, break also, and may we be swept away,
forever to regret our dishonour.

5 - The Secret of Tora

Lief stared at the dead and broken rock, his heart sinking as at last he remembered the words from *The Belt of Deltora* that described the powers of the emerald.

† **The emerald, symbol of honor, dulls in the presence of evil, and when a vow is broken.**

He needed no further proof of what had happened. "Tora broke its vow," he murmured. "But why? Why?"

With a groan of frustration and disappointment, Barda moved away. But Lief and Jasmine could not follow him. Not yet.

Lief put his hand upon Dain's shoulder. "Get up, Dain," he said quietly. "There is nothing for you here. Nothing for any of us. Tora is empty. Everything is preserved by enchantment, but it is empty of life. It has been so, I think, for a very long time. That is why the lake silted up, and the city was cut off from the river."

But Dain shook his head miserably. "It cannot be," he whispered. "I have waited so long." His face was drawn and deeply shadowed. His whole body trembled.

Jasmine knelt beside him. "Dain, why did you have to come to Tora? Tell us the truth!"

Dain's voice was very low. "I thought my parents were here. Mother told me, always, that if ever we were separated, they would meet me in Tora. She said she had family here, and they would shelter us."

His fists clenched. "I told Doom this, a year ago, when he found me left for dead by the bandits who attacked our farm. He said to tell no one, because when my parents arrived in Tora they would be in danger if it became known that their son was with the Resistance."

"How could it become known?" Lief demanded.

"Doom fears there is a spy in our camp. At least — that is what he told me." Dain looked up at the ruined stone, his eyes bitter. "But he also told me that Tora was filled with spies, and overrun by Grey Guards and Ols. He was lying. All the time he delayed me, making false promises, he knew that the city was deserted, and that my hopes for it were false."

He took a deep, shuddering breath. "I will never go back to the stronghold. Never."

He bowed his head and did not raise it again. Lief looked at him. Dimly he realized that at one time he might have been irritated because Dain blamed Doom for all his troubles. For, after all, Dain had not been Doom's prisoner. He could at anytime have left the Resistance and travelled to Tora alone.

But Lief did not feel irritated now. Only filled with a calm regret. Briefly he wondered about that.

"Look here!"

Barda's voice sounded strange. Lief looked up and saw that his friend had climbed the steps of the great hall. Behind him, graceful white columns reached for the sky, but he was looking down, at the open, carved box in his hands.

"Go," said Jasmine in a low voice. "I will stay here."

Lief rose, crossed the square, and climbed the steps. Barda held out the box for him to see. Inside were countless small rolls of parchment. Lief picked one out, and unrolled it.

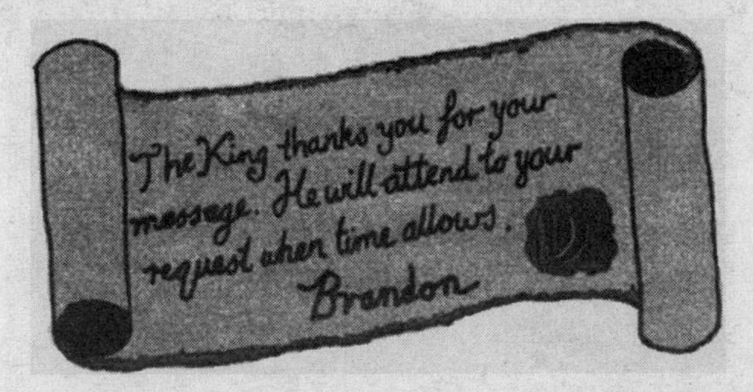
The King thanks you for your message. He will attend to your request when time allows.
Brandon

Lief scrambled through the box, picking up other rolls and looking at them. They were all the same, except for the signatures. Some were signed by Queen

Lilia, others by King Alton, Endon's father. Still others bore the name of Endon himself.

"These are like the messages Father showed me," said Lief dully. "The messages the people of Del received when they sent requests and complaints to the king."

Barda nodded. "It seems that the Torans also sent requests and complaints, and received the same replies. I imagine that like the people of Del they felt they had been abandoned. So when the last message came . . ."

He handed Lief two crumpled scraps of paper. "These were in the box also," he said heavily. "On top of all the rest."

The scraps were the two halves of a note. Lief fitted the halves together and read the hastily scribbled message.

People of Tora:

The Belt of Deltora is lost, the Shadow Lord has returned. With the help of a true friend, I have escaped with the Queen and our unborn child. I ask you to offer sanctuary in fulfilment of your ancient vow. Return word by this messenger.

Waste no time, I beg you.

Endon
King of Deltora

Lief stared at the note. "Messenger? What messenger?" he stammered.

"A bird, no doubt," said Barda. "A blackbird like Kree, almost certainly. Once they were plentiful in Del, and in olden times they were always thought of as the King's birds, because of their cleverness. That is probably why the Sorceress Thaegan so hated them, and relished eating them."

"The Torans tore the note apart," breathed Lief. "They refused help, and broke the vow. How could they risk so much?"

Barda shrugged. His face was heavy, grey with disappointment. "The stone in the square dates from the time of Adin. Perhaps the Torans no longer believed in the words. But the ancient magic was still powerful. The moment they tore up the note, they were doomed."

He looked down at the carved box in his hands. "This was something your father did not count on, Lief. The king and queen left Del in haste, long before any return message could have been expected from Tora. No doubt they thought they would receive word as they travelled, and Toran magic to help them on their way. But the plan failed."

"So all this time Father has believed that the heir was safe in Tora, waiting for us," Lief murmured. "That was his secret. He thought we would meet here, and early in our travels, too. Do you remember? His plan was for the Valley of the Lost to be our first goal, not our last. If it had been, we would surely have passed Tora on our way to the Maze of the Beast."

He put his hands on the Belt. It gave him courage.

"The plan to hide in Tora may have failed, but somehow Endon and Sharn found another place of safety," he said. "The Belt is whole. Father told us that means the heir lives, wherever he may be. When the Belt is complete, it will show us the way. Father told us it would. We must believe him."

He put the two halves of the note back into the carved box, closed the lid firmly, and put the box back on the step.

When he looked up, Barda was frowning, his gaze sweeping around the great square and the buildings that surrounded it, the great columns, the statues of birds and beasts, the carved urns overflowing with flowers. Lief wondered what he was doing. Except for the cracked stone, where Dain still huddled, locked in his private misery, and Jasmine crouched beside him, there was nothing to see.

"If the city is empty, why is it still so perfect and whole, Lief?" Barda asked suddenly. "Why have looters and scavengers not destroyed it? The pirates, the bandits . . . what has stopped them from plundering this place at their will?"

He pointed at the box. "Even that is a work of art. It would be of great value to a trader. No doubt the city is full of such things. Yet no one has stolen them. Why?"

He spoke softly, but still the square seemed to echo with his voice.

Lief felt a chill run up his spine. "You think Tora is — protected?" he whispered.

"Lief! Barda!" called Jasmine.

Startled, they looked down. Jasmine was still crouching beside Dain. She beckoned urgently, and they ran back down the stairs and across the square to her side.

Dain did not raise his head, though he must have heard them come. Jasmine had wrapped a blanket around him, but still he trembled.

"He will not move," whispered Jasmine fearfully. "He cannot stop shaking, and will not take any water. I am very afraid for him."

Dain's pale lips opened. "Take me away from here, I beg you," he mumbled. "I cannot bear it. Please — take me away."

6 - The Newcomers

With Lief and Barda supporting Dain between them, the companions began to make their way out of the city. Dain's eyes were dark and blank. His feet stumbled and dragged. Cold sweat beaded his brow. The terrible shuddering still racked his slight body.

Lief was sorry to see his suffering, but somewhere in the back of his mind he wondered at Dain's collapse. Had the boy not trained with Doom and the Resistance for a year? Had he not faced Ols and other terrible dangers as part of everyday life?

Dain had hoped to find his parents in Tora, and he had not. But how could this shock and disappointment fell him so completely? It was as though his heart was broken like Tora's stone, and the light of his spirit had been snuffed out like the green fire.

They walked on, all but Dain glancing from side

to side at the houses they passed. Clearly visible through gleaming windows were the sad signs of vanished life: food as fresh as the day it was made, wonderfully painted plates and dishes, embroidered cushions and hangings. In almost every house there was a weaver's loom on which cloth of miraculous fineness hung waiting for the long-vanished weaver to return.

The looms reminded Lief of his mother. How often had he seen her sit weaving cloth for their garments and household needs? Lief knew that his mother's skill was great, because other people had told him so. But the threads she had to use were coarse and dull — nothing like the threads of Tora, which glowed like jewels.

The finest thing she had ever made was the cloak he now wore. Into that she had put her greatest skill. And love and memories besides, she had said.

Where was his mother now?

I, of all people, should understand Dain's grief, Lief thought. I know what it is to miss and fear for well-loved parents.

But you have not given up hope, a voice in the back of his mind whispered. You have not abandoned yourself to despair and become ill in body and mind. And did Jasmine give in and die when her parents were taken? Did Barda despair when his mother was killed and his friends were slaughtered?

Lief shook his head, to drive the voice away. People have different strengths and weaknesses, he told himself. I should not blame —

His thoughts took a different turn as another idea came to him. Perhaps there was something else behind Dain's collapse that he did not yet understand. All the signs were that the boy was not simply grieved and disappointed, but deeply shocked. More shocked than was reasonable, if he had told the whole truth.

The entrance tunnel was before them. They entered its cool shade and once again Lief felt that mysterious tingling run through his body. He walked in a dream, moving out into the sun with regret.

He and Barda lowered Dain gently to the ground. The boy lay shivering as if with cold, his great eyes staring sightlessly at the bright sky.

"Dain, you must try to be strong," Barda urged softly. "You are making yourself ill."

He said the words several times, and at last Dain responded. Slowly the blank eyes came back into focus. The boy swallowed, and wet his dry lips.

"I am sorry," he murmured. "Finding the city empty . . . was a great shock. But that is no excuse."

Kree screeched, flapping his wings warningly.

"Someone is coming!" Jasmine exclaimed, drawing her dagger.

Lief looked across the lake, but it remained still. The danger was coming by land, then. From the hills that rose beside and beyond the city.

Kree soared upward, preparing to investigate.

"No, Kree!" Jasmine cried. "They may have bows and arrows. Stay with us."

The bird hovered for a moment, then reluctantly came back to earth.

"Jasmine, are there many?" snapped Barda.

As she had done so often before, Jasmine knelt and put her ear to the ground. "Only two, I think," she said after a moment. "Both tall. One heavier than the other."

Dain was watching her intently, plainly very impressed. Lief saw that the trembling in the boy's limbs had eased. Having something else to think about seems to be just what Dain needs, he thought. But he found that he was slightly annoyed.

Yet why should Dain not admire Jasmine? he thought, turning his irritation on himself. Anyone would admire her skill! Then it occurred to him that if he was still inside Tora he would not be angry, but quite calm.

The city's spell is wearing off, he thought. I am almost back to normal.

And at last he understood what the tingling in the tunnel had meant. He understood why Tora remained perfect and untouched after over sixteen years of emptiness.

"Lief!" growled Barda. "Quickly!"

Lief drew his sword and hurried to join his friends. They were standing shoulder to shoulder, making a barrier between Dain and two tall figures approaching from the hills. The figures seemed to shimmer in the dazzling sunlight.

Were they bandits? Ols?

"Tora is protected by magic," Lief said rapidly. "Magic that works on hearts and minds. The tunnel drains away all evil. If we return there, nothing can harm us."

Barda glanced at him quickly, then back at the city's shining walls. Lief could see that he was measuring the distance in his mind, trying to decide if they should risk turning and making a dash for safety. But it was too late. The strangers had seen them, and quickened their pace.

Dain began crawling unsteadily to his feet.

"Dain — go back to Tora," Barda ordered. But Dain shook his head stubbornly, feeling for his dagger.

"Dain!" Jasmine exclaimed. "Go!"

"If they are Ols, I can help," Dain said, through gritted teeth. "I will stand with you, or die. I have had enough of weakness."

He moved into place beside her and frowned at the approaching strangers. Then suddenly his eyes narrowed. His mouth firmed to a hard line.

"Doom!" he muttered, and turned away.

Startled, Lief, Barda, and Jasmine realized that he was right. Now they could see that the taller of the approaching strangers was the man who called himself Doom of the Hills. Doom, who they had last seen in the Resistance stronghold. Who had held them prisoner for three long days.

To their amazement they saw that Neridah the Swift was with him. Why had he chosen her as a companion? As they drew closer, Lief could see that Neridah's lips were curved into a smile. But Doom's face was stern.

"Do not relax!" muttered Barda. "They could be Ols, trying to deceive us."

Plainly, Dain thought not, and Lief did not, either. But still his hand tightened on the hilt of his sword. Doom had shown himself to be as dangerous as any Ol, in his way. He was not to be trusted.

When he reached them, Doom wasted no words on greetings. "So, Dain," he growled. "You are where you wanted to be. Are you satisfied?"

"You knew!" Dain burst out. "You knew all along what Tora was, Doom. You lied to me!"

"Of course," said Doom coolly. "For what else was keeping you strong but hope? Has seeing that your hope was in vain made you feel better, or worse?"

Dain's face clearly showed the answer. Doom nodded bitterly. "Ever since you came to the stronghold I have been seeking your parents, Dain. I had hoped to be successful before you could find out that they were not in Tora. But you could not wait."

"No, I could not!" cried Dain defiantly. "But that

is not my fault. I did not know the truth of things. I am not a child, to be protected and fed with fairy tales! You drove me to what I did by deceiving me!"

Doom stared at him for a long moment. Then, surprisingly, his grim face relaxed into what could have been a smile. "Once you would not have spoken to your elders that way," he said. "Such a polite, obedient child you were, when first I met you."

"I am not a child!" Dain shouted furiously.

"No, it seems you are not. Perhaps . . ." Doom seemed to ponder. "Perhaps I was wrong." His lips twitched. "It does not happen often. But it is possible. If I beg your pardon, will you come back to the stronghold with us? You are sorely missed."

Dain hesitated, swaying uncertainly.

Barda, Lief, and Jasmine glanced at one another. In all their minds was the thought that many problems would be solved if Dain agreed to go with Doom. But they had to be sure he would be safe.

Lief stepped forward. "We have learned, since seeing you last, that it is not wise to trust appearances, Doom," he said in a level voice. "Before Dain decides what he wishes to do we would like you, and Neridah, too, to go into Tora."

Doom's dark eyes turned on him. And now there was no warmth or humor in them.

"You need not stay more than a moment," Lief

went on, refusing to be cowed. "The Tora tunnel discovers evil far more quickly than your Testing Room."

"So — you have discovered Tora's secret!" sneered Doom. "Congratulations! But what if I refuse to agree to your request? What then?"

7 - A Battle of Wills

Neridah moved to stand beside Doom. Barda and Jasmine stepped into place beside Lief. The two sides glared at one another. Then Barda spoke.

"If you refuse to go into Tora, then we must assume that you are Ols, and act accordingly."

Doom's sword was in his hand in an instant.

"No!" shouted Dain, thrusting himself in front of Barda. "You must not fight! You are not enemies, but on the same side!"

Doom's face did not change. "I am still not sure of that," he said grimly.

"And neither are we, twice over!" Jasmine exclaimed. "For if you are really the man Doom, you have treated us badly and we do not trust you. And if you are an Ol in Doom's shape, you are a danger to us all."

Doom's eyes flickered. Plainly, he could see the sense in Jasmine's words. Yet still he did not lower his sword.

"How can it harm you to prove to us that you are what you seem?" Lief murmured, deliberately keeping his voice low and even.

"We do not have to prove anything to you!" Neridah cried angrily. "Doom and I have been together since we left the stronghold. We can swear — "

Doom put out a hand to quiet her. "What we swear proves nothing, Neridah," he said. "Ols most often travel in pairs, do they not?"

Then, as if Neridah's interruption had somehow helped him to make up his mind, he shrugged, sheathed his sword and began to stride towards the city's shimmering light. Neridah, plainly surprised and angry, hesitated, glaring for a moment, then swung around and stalked after him.

The companions followed. When they reached the tunnel they waited as Doom and Neridah went on alone. Lief had been tempted to enter the tunnel, too, but somehow knew that this would not be wise. He could not afford all his passions to drain away at this moment. A little anger kept one alert. And one could not be too alert when dealing with one such as Doom.

So he stood and watched, and saw what he otherwise might not have seen. As the two figures walked through the tunnel, the air began to fill with colored sparks, swirling like dust motes lit by the sun.

"I saw nothing of that when we walked through," breathed Jasmine. "I only — felt."

"It must be invisible to those who are inside." Barda rubbed his hand over his dazzled eyes and turned away.

In seconds Doom and Neridah had disappeared in a cloud of dancing light. But in only a few more moments they became visible again, walking slowly back the way they had come.

As they stepped out into the sunlight, both seemed dazed. Their faces were smooth and strangely still.

"So — you are satisfied now, I hope?" Doom said. But the words held no sting, and his eyes looked lost. Groaning, he sat down, his back against the city wall.

Neridah, Dain, and the others stared at him in confusion. Wearily, he looked up.

"When anger, hatred, and bitterness have left a man who lives by little else, what is there left for him but emptiness?" he asked with a slight smile. "That is why I do not enjoy visiting Tora. I have done so only once before — and that was enough."

"Who are you, Doom?" asked Lief suddenly.

For a moment he thought the man would not answer. Then Doom's shoulders slumped and his eyes closed, as though he did not have the strength to refuse.

"I do not know who I am," he said. "I do not know what I have lost, along with my name. My memories begin in the Shadowlands. I was fighting a Vraal in the Shadow Arena. I was injured. Everything before that is darkness."

His hand moved slowly to the jagged scar on his face.

"But you escaped?" Lief prompted. Perhaps it was cruel to use Doom's present weakness to find out more about him. But it was a chance that would not come again.

"I escaped the Shadow Arena," Doom went on. "They were not expecting that. They thought I was finished. I fled across the mountains, pursued and with no clear idea of anything save that Deltora was my home. On Dread Mountain I turned and faced my pursuers. I escaped once more, but it cost me dearly."

He sighed deeply. "I travelled on, more dead than alive. At last I was found, given shelter, and healed by a good man."

"A man who lived in a place called Kinrest," murmured Jasmine.

Doom glanced at her, and again he smiled, though his eyes were filled with sadness. "So you have seen his grave, and know I took his name," he said. "He saved me, but I brought death to him. The Grey Guards who had not died on the Mountain pursued me to his cave. Doom was a man of peace. He had no chance against them. But thanks to him I was strong once more. I killed them all, and scattered their bones."

A touch of the old savagery was in his voice as he spoke those last words. Lief realized that the calming effect of the Toran tunnel was gradually wearing off. Doom was silent for a moment, and when next he smiled, it was merely a bitter tweak of the lips.

"You have taken advantage of me, I fear," he said, climbing to his feet. "I hope your curiosity is satisfied." His mouth was tightening, his eyes darkening. The grim, familiar mask was settling back onto his face.

"Doom, I knew you had been through much," breathed Neridah. "But I had no idea . . ." Her voice trailed off as Doom shot her a cold look. Plainly he did not want her sympathy or her admiration. Her face reddened. Then she tossed her head angrily and moved away from them.

"I did not pry into your affairs out of simple curiosity, Doom," said Lief in a low voice.

"No?" Doom looked into his eyes for a long moment. Then he turned to Dain. "I am due to meet Steven the peddler in a few days," he said flatly. "He has new supplies for us. Will you come with me? Or do you choose to remain with your new friends?"

"There is no choice, Doom. Dain must go with you," Barda said quickly. "We have a hard, long journey ahead of us."

Dain's sensitive skin flushed red. "I do not want to be a burden to anyone," he said through stiff lips. "I will go with you, Doom, to meet Steven."

Doom nodded shortly. Then, as though despite himself he resented having Dain so easily cast aside, he lifted one eyebrow. "And where are you travelling, that your journey is going to be so hard?" he demanded.

Even long afterwards, Lief did not know why he said what he did then. It was the impulse of a moment. Perhaps he felt the urge to give Doom some information, as a sign of trust. Or perhaps it was simply that he was tired of lies.

"We are going to the Valley of the Lost," he said clearly.

Barda and Jasmine turned to him, astonished that he should speak so freely. Dain looked curious. But Doom nodded, his face darkening.

"I thought it might be so," he said. "And I warn you with all my heart to turn your faces from the plan. The Valley is not for such as you."

"What do you know of it?" growled Barda.

Doom looked over to where Neridah sat looking out over the waters of the lake, and lowered his voice.

"It is an evil place. A place of misery and lost souls. I know of many who have entered it, seeking the great jewel that is its Guardian's prize."

Lief glanced quickly at Barda and Jasmine. Both looked startled and watchful. He wet his lips.

"A great jewel?" he asked carefully.

Doom looked at him with something like scorn. "Do not insult me by trying to pretend. I know it is your goal. A diamond, it is said, larger and more powerful than any ever seen. Beautiful. Pure. Priceless."

He shook his head. "It is no secret in these parts. Its fame has lured many before you into the Guardian's clutches. All entered the valley in hope. All came to wish bitterly that they had never seen it."

8 – A Parting of the Ways

Lief felt a chill of fear, but straightened his shoulders. Barda stood like a rock, his hand on his sword. But Jasmine tossed back her hair and lifted her chin. "Still, we must go," she said.

Doom reached forward and gripped her shoulders. *"You must not!"* he hissed between clenched teeth. "Listen to me! Your quest is already lost. If you persist, you will be lost also. And for what? For a dream! For nothing!"

Jasmine shook herself free and drew back so that she, Lief, and Barda were standing shoulder to shoulder. Doom stared at them for a moment, then raised his hands and dropped them again, in surrender.

"I have done my best," he muttered. "I can do no more. But it is a waste. Already you have a following. Together we might have roused the people. We might have stood united against the Shadow Lord. We might have saved Deltora."

"For now, we must go our separate ways, it is true," said Barda. "But when the time is right, we will join the fight together."

"When the time is right . . ." Doom turned away. "I fear that time will never come for you, my friends. Not now."

Grim-faced, he slung his pack on his shoulder and jerked his head to Dain. "Tell Neridah we are leaving," he ordered. "I have already wasted too much time here, and Steven will not wait."

With a backward glance at Lief, Barda, and Jasmine, Dain trudged unsteadily to the water's edge.

"You know more than you are telling, Doom!" exclaimed Jasmine. "If you can help us, you should do so!"

Doom shook his head. "You have refused the only help I can give you," he muttered. "You have no right to ask more."

He frowned down at her from his great height. She looked up at him, her green eyes snapping with anger. Then, quite suddenly, he gave a short laugh.

"There is one thing I can do for you," he said. He pulled a dark woollen cap from his pocket, and tossed it to her. "You and the bird are what make your party recognizable. Cover your hair with this. You are already dressed as a boy, and a ragged boy at that. Your hair is all that gives you away."

Jasmine glared, as if uncertain whether to accept the gift or not, but finally her sense overcame her pride. She twisted up her hair and bundled on the cap, pulling it down around her ears. Instantly she was transformed. It was as though a scowling young boy stood before them.

Kree squawked. Plainly, he did not like the change. But Doom nodded. "That is better," he said.

He turned as Dain approached, and frowned again as he saw that the boy was alone. "Why is Neridah not with you?" he snapped.

"She — she will not come," Dain stammered. "She says she has decided to travel on, to her home."

Doom snorted angrily. "So that is why she insisted on coming with me! I am sure she never intended to return. Life in the stronghold does not suit her. It is too hard, too dangerous, and there is no money to spare for the luxuries a spoiled athlete has grown used to."

"But — is she not afraid the Grey Guards will track her down?" asked Lief.

"No doubt she thinks that she will be able to persuade you to escort her at least part of the way. And she is convinced that once she reaches home, she will be safe," Doom shook his head. "She is a fool! Another fool who will not take heed of warnings."

Without another word he turned and began

striding away towards the hills. Dain hesitated for a moment, then murmured a hurried farewell, and went after him.

*

As Doom had predicted, Neridah did her best to persuade the companions to let her accompany them. At last she broke down and cried in Barda's arms, wailing that she had left the Resistance only because Doom had broken her heart.

"I love him," she sobbed. "But he is cruel, and cares nothing for me. I cannot stay where I see him every day. I cannot!"

Barda patted her shoulder awkwardly. But Jasmine regarded her with cold surprise and Lief — Lief knew enough of Neridah's deceiving ways to wonder how real her tears were.

At last, at Barda's urging, they agreed to let her travel with them for a day or two. "But after that, we must separate, Neridah," Barda warned her gently. "Our goal is a dread and dangerous place."

"The Valley of the Lost," Neridah whispered. "I know. I heard its name, when you were speaking with Doom. You are so brave — braver by far than Doom realizes."

Again, Lief wondered about her. She had shown no sign that she had heard what they were talking about with Doom. She had sat quite still, staring out at the lake as if lost in thought. And all the time she had been listening. She had heard the name of the Valley of the Lost. What else had she heard?

She is sly, he thought. We must be careful of her.

⁜

In the end, Neridah travelled with them for nearly a week. She protested strongly about travelling by night, and was a sulky and complaining companion. But though they passed many roads that led in the direction of her home, she refused to take them. Whenever Lief, Barda, and Jasmine tried to part with her, she cried and ran after them. She clung to them like honey, and at last she lost even Barda's sympathy.

"I have begun to think that she is not being truthful with us," he whispered one day, as Neridah sulked in her sleeping blanket. "She said she wished to go home. Why does she not do so?"

"I do not know," Lief whispered back. "But we must do something about her quickly. I do not trust her, and I do not want her with us when we reach the Valley of the Lost. According to the map, and our reckoning, it is not far from here."

"She will not willingly let us go on without her, that is certain," Jasmine said grimly. "So we have two choices. One, hit her on the head, and run. Or, two, wait until we are sure that she is asleep, then creep away."

She seemed a little disappointed when Lief and Barda chose the second course.

A few hours later they carried out the plan, sneaking away from the camping place like thieves. They walked fast all day, trying to keep under cover, and at sunset reached a range of steep, thickly wooded hills.

"The valley is within this range, I am sure of it," said Barda.

Lief looked up at the hills. "It will be a long, hard climb," he sighed. "And dangerous, for the woods are thick, and it will be very dark. The moon tonight is at its smallest. And tomorrow night there will be no moon at all."

Jasmine pulled off her cap impatiently. "I can hear nothing with this thick wool over my ears!" she complained, shaking her hair free with relief. "Now — what were you saying? That it would be dark tonight? And that the woods are thick? Quite so. I suggest we sleep the night through, for once, knowing that we can climb in the morning, well hidden by the trees."

The plan seemed an excellent one. They did exactly as Jasmine suggested. So it was not until the close of the following day that they reached the top of that ragged hill and looked down at the jagged crack in the earth that was the Valley of the Lost.

9 - The Valley of the Lost

A thick grey mist crawled sullenly on the valley floor. It lapped to the very tops of the trees, stirred by the slow movements of half-seen figures that thronged the depths. A faint, damp warmth smelling of green decay, of rotting wood, and of smothered life, brushed the friends' faces like an echo of the mist.

Jasmine fidgeted. Filli was chattering into her ear. Kree, after a single clucking chirp, sat motionless on her arm. "They do not like the valley," she murmured.

"I cannot say that I am entranced by it, either," said Barda dryly.

Jasmine hunched her shoulders and shivered. Then, without another word, she turned and returned to the largest of the trees that ringed the lip of the cliff. In amazement, Lief and Barda watched her lift Filli from her shoulder and put him onto the highest branch she could reach. Kree fluttered up beside him.

"I know you will take care of one another," Jasmine said. "Keep safe."

She turned and, without looking back, walked back to Lief and Barda. She met their questioning eyes calmly. "I told you," she said. "Kree and Filli do not like the valley. They cannot go there."

"Why?" Lief burst out. He looked down to where Kree and Filli still perched on their branch, staring after Jasmine forlornly.

Jasmine shrugged. "If they go there they will die," she said simply. "The valley is not for them. Or any creature. The mist will kill them."

A shiver ran down Lief's back. "What about us?" he asked abruptly.

"There are people down there. I can see their shadows in the mist," said Jasmine. "And if they can survive, so can we. We will go down to where the mist begins. Then we will decide what to do."

Abruptly, she swung around and held up her hand to Filli and Kree. Then she turned once more, pulled her cap more firmly over her ears, and scrambled over the edge of the cliff.

Lief and Barda followed. The ground beneath their feet was steep and treacherous, slippery with loose stones. Half walking, half sliding, always in danger of falling, they moved down and down. After only a few minutes, Lief lost the sense that he was walking of his own accord. The slippery stones, the steepness of the slope, were doing all the work for him. From the cliff edge, the valley floor had seemed very far away. Now it was growing closer by the moment.

Once, he looked back. The cliff-top towered high above them. Impossibly high. Impossibly far away. It was hard to believe he and his friends had ever stood there. Hard to believe that they had ever had the choice of descending, staying where they were, or even turning their backs and walking away from the valley.

For now it seemed that there was no choice. The closer they moved to the crawling mist, the more it seemed to draw them, and the steeper the slope became. It took far more energy to stand still than to move on. The companions clutched one another for support, but they could do little to help one another.

And before they realized it, the mist was around them. It was as if it had risen to meet them, brushing their faces with warm, damp fingers, casting a haze over their eyes. Slowly it stole into their mouths and noses, filling them with its oversweet scent, its taste of decay.

This was not the plan, Lief thought in confusion. He tried to stop in mid-stride, then slipped and fell, rolling blindly, gasping and scrambling on the stones. He heard Jasmine and Barda calling him in alarm, but could do nothing to save himself.

When finally he came to a stop, he realized that he was on the valley floor. The mist swirled thick about him. Shadowy trees, thick with mold, hung with vines, stretched above his head. Great clumps of glistening dark red fungus bulged from twisted roots beside his face. Lush ferns arched around him, brushing his face and his hands as he scrambled, panting, to his feet.

And everywhere there was a soft sighing, like wind in the trees. But there was no wind. The sound seemed to come from everywhere, from all around him, out of the swirling greyness where darker shadows slipped and writhed, moving closer.

"Barda! Jasmine!" Lief shouted, gripped with sudden terror. But the mist muffled his voice so that it sounded thin and piping. And when his friends answered, their voices sounded far, far away.

He called again. He thought he heard a cry of pain, and his stomach lurched. But then he saw his friends stumbling towards him out of the gloom. He lurched forward, gripping their arms thankfully.

"Well, we are still alive, in any case," growled Barda. "The mist has not killed us yet."

But Jasmine said nothing. She had drawn her dagger and was standing very still, every muscle tense.

The sighing, whispering sound was louder. The mist around them stirred and billowed, the shadows deepening, closing in.

"Keep back!" Jasmine hissed, raising her dagger menacingly.

The shadows seemed to falter, but only for an instant. Then they pressed forward again. And now Lief could see that they were people, crowds of men, women, and children coming through the mist, from all directions.

They did not look unfriendly. Indeed, their pale faces seemed filled with timid eagerness and welcome as they drifted forward, long, thin hands stretched out towards the companions. Their fingers were pale grey, almost transparent, and so were the long clothes that fluttered around them and the hair that hung lank down their backs. No wonder they had seemed part of the mist.

They whispered as they moved, the sound of their voices like dry leaves rustling in the wind, but Lief could understand nothing of what they said. Yet he did not feel threatened. Even when they came very close, and the first of them began touching his face, clothes, and hair with fingers that felt dry and light as moths' wings, he felt no thrill of fear, only a shrinking distaste.

And still more of the people came, and more. The colorless rags they wore hung around limbs that seemed just skin and bone. Their shapes seemed to blend and mingle, overlapping as they pressed in, each hand moving upon a dozen others, touching, stroking . . .

Barda and Lief stood rigidly still. But Jasmine quivered, her mouth set and her eyes screwed shut.

"I cannot bear this," she whispered. "Who are they? What is wrong with them?" Her dagger hung loosely in her hand. She made no move to use it. She could not do so. The people were so plainly harmless, so plainly in some sort of terrible need.

There was a stir in the crowd. It swayed and shivered like a field of long grass swept by the wind. Then the fluttering hands were slipping away, and the people were backing, whispering, into the mist, their grey eyes filled with hopeless longing.

There was fear in the air. Lief could feel it. Almost smell it. Then he saw its source. A tall, dark shadow, pierced by two points of red light that glowed like burning coals, was coming through the mist towards them.

He tried to put his hand on his sword. But his hand would not move. He tried to step back. But his feet would not obey him. A single glance told him that Barda and Jasmine were under the same spell.

The shadow gathered form and shape. Now Lief could see that the red coals were eyes, eyes that burned in the ravaged face of a tall, bearded man wearing a long, dark robe. The man held two thick grey cords in each of his hands. They stretched away into the mist behind him, as though they were attached to something, but he paid no attention to them.

His burning eyes were fixed on Lief, Barda, and Jasmine.

They struggled to free themselves, and his thin lips curved into a smile that was full of malice.

"Do not waste your strength," he purred. "You can do nothing unless I will it. As you will learn, in time. Welcome to my valley. It has been a long time since I have had the pleasure of visitors. And now I am blessed with four."

He watched with keen pleasure as Lief, Barda, and Jasmine glanced at one another in surprise. *Four* visitors? What did he mean?

"Perhaps you thought to trick me by splitting your party, did you?" he said. "Ah, that is what I like to see. Visitors who like games. That will make things so much more pleasant, for all of us."

He crooked a bony finger. And to the companions' amazement, out of the mist stumbled Neridah, her bewildered face bruised and bleeding.

She had stubbornly followed them, despite everything they had done! Now they had her to worry about, as well as themselves. Gritting his teeth in anger, Lief remembered the cry he had heard. No doubt Neridah had tripped coming down the steep slope alone.

He glanced at the woman in helpless irritation as she staggered to a halt beside him. But Neridah did not look at him. She was staring straight ahead, her eyes dark with fear and confusion.

Their tormentor was rubbing his hands.

"Who are you?" Lief demanded.

The man smiled mockingly.

"I?" he purred. "Why, have you not guessed? I am the Guardian."

With a swirl of his robes, he turned and began walking away into the mist. Just before the companions lost sight of him, he carelessly lifted one hand and crooked the index finger.

And, unable to help themselves, feet dragging as they fought to resist his command, Neridah, Lief, Jasmine, and Barda stumbled after him.

10 - The Palace

The mist swirled about them as they walked. Ferns and vines brushed their legs and faces. Shadows flickered at the edge of their vision. The valley's people were watching, but not daring to come near.

In front of them strode the Guardian, straight-backed and tall.

"If this Guardian is taking us to his cave, or hut, or wherever he lives, so much the better," whispered Jasmine. "That will be where he keeps — "

She broke off, glancing at Neridah, who tossed her head angrily. "I know about the great diamond!" she said, in a high voice. "Why do you think I followed you here? For the sake of your fine company?"

She stared fearfully at the Guardian's back. "I thought you would be bound to succeed, no matter who else had failed," she went on, her voice trembling. "I did not dream that you would have us captured and helpless within moments of setting foot in the valley!"

"We have been captured before, and saved ourselves," hissed Jasmine. "We will do it again. We still have our weapons."

"He spoke of games," Lief said slowly. "He likes games. What do you think he means?"

Barda grimaced. "Nothing pleasant, in any case. But surely it proves, at least, that he is a man, not an Ol or some other beast in human shape. It is humans who like games."

"And if he is only a man we can defeat him, for all his magic," said Jasmine. "Defeat him, and take the gem. We have only to wait, and learn his weaknesses."

Lief hesitated. He, too, believed that the Guardian was human beneath the trappings of his magic power. But he was not so sure that this would make their task any easier. And something was still nagging at his memory. Something that made his skin prickle with warning whenever he thought of the diamond.

They walked for what seemed a long time, crossing a deep stream and moving at last into a clearing. Abruptly, the Guardian stopped and held up his hand. Lights began to glow through the mist. As the companions drew closer, they saw that the lights were shining inside a domed glass palace.

Mist tumbled outside the glass walls, shining

eerily in the reflected light. Hundreds of shadowy grey figures shuffled in the haze. But within the palace, rich colors glowed. The many rooms were full of fine furniture, bright rugs and paintings, gold and silver statues, silken cushions and hangings. The whole glittered like a jewel.

The Guardian had stood aside so that his prisoners could better see the palace's wonder. Now he smiled proudly at their astonished faces.

"A dwelling fit for a king, you will agree," he said.

When none of them answered him, his smile disappeared and a scowl took its place.

"We will go inside," he snapped. "Perhaps that will loosen your tongues and make you more agreeable." He tugged the cords that he held in his hands and four shapes lumbered from behind him, out of the mist.

Lief heard Neridah gasp. And indeed his own breath caught in his throat as he saw the creatures emerging from the swirling grey.

Hairless, gross, and misshapen, covered in sores and boils, twisted arms hanging almost to the ground, the monsters grinned and slobbered as they stared at the prisoners. The rubbery cords that bound them to their master coiled from puffy red centers in the backs of their necks. Sickened, Lief realized that the cords were part of them. Flesh of their flesh.

"Here are my pets — my companions," said the

Guardian. "I have kept them hidden until now, not wishing to alarm you. But you will learn to love them, as I have done. Perhaps you already do so, though you do not know it. They are fine, strong monsters, are they not? They protect me, and keep me company. Their names are Pride, Envy, Hate, and Greed."

As he spoke, he lightly flicked the monsters on the head one by one. The moment it felt his touch, each creature swayed and groaned with pleasure.

The Guardian smiled. "Their names are a little joke of mine," he said. "For though each has one of the faults I have mentioned, none has that fault after which it is named. Greed is not greedy, Pride is not proud, Envy is not envious. Hate is not envious, either, not at all. But more important, it has never hated in its life. You see? Is that not amusing?"

Again receiving no reply, he turned and walked to a door set into one of the palace walls. The door swung open and he stood back.

Lief, Barda, Jasmine, and Neridah at once found themselves moving to the door. In a moment they were inside the palace, and the Guardian was following. The monsters crowded after him, grunting, their leads flopping horribly from their necks. In the crush, three of them began to snarl and claw at one another.

Their master barked an angry command, kicking out at them savagely. When at last they had quietened, he turned back to the companions.

"Like children, my pets sometimes do not agree,

and need a firm hand," he said smoothly. "The envious one and the proud one are both very afraid of Greed. But they will fight if they have to. For, after all, they are linked together and cannot escape."

The door swung shut with a soft click.

Lief looked around, blinking in the bright light. The room they had entered was vast, and furnished with every luxury. A fountain splashed and sparkled in its center. Velvet cushions lay in heaps upon the shining floor. Soft music played, though Lief could not see where the sound was coming from.

At one end of the room was a long table draped in a white cloth and gleaming with silver and crystal. Long white candles burned in exquisite candlesticks among dishes full of steaming, fragrant food.

Five places had been laid. Two on each side of the table, one at the head.

The Guardian rubbed his hands with a dry, rasping sound. "So — now we are alone," he said. "Now we can enjoy each other's company. Fine food and drink. Music. Conversation. And, later, perhaps, the game."

*

The food looked and smelled delicious, but to the companions it tasted like dust and ashes, and they ate little. They spoke little, too, for it was clear from the beginning that what their host wanted was not a conversation, but an audience.

His voice flowed on as he sat at the head of the

table, his hideous pets squatting behind his chair. The leads, Lief saw, were attached to his wrists, no doubt by bands hidden under his sleeves. This way, his hands could be free while the beasts remained under his control.

"I was born to great riches, but through the wickedness and envy of others I lost everything," he said, pouring golden wine into a crystal goblet. "I was driven out of my home. No one would raise a hand to help me. Alone, grieving, despairing, and despised, I took refuge in this valley. My only companions at first were the birds and other small creatures. But — "

"There are no birds or small creatures in this valley," Jasmine broke in. "Or none that I have seen."

The Guardian glanced at her under his eyebrows, plainly annoyed by the interruption. "They have gone," he snapped. "They had no place here once I was transformed, and the valley became the Valley of the Lost."

He leaned forward, his red eyes gleaming hotly in the candlelight. "Do you not want to know how this miracle occurred?" he demanded. "Do you not want to know how I, an outcast, gained new wealth, a new kingdom, and powers a thousand times greater than those I had lost?"

He did not wait for them to answer, but continued as though there had been no interruption.

"A voice spoke to me as I sat grieving. It whispered to me night and day. It reminded me of how I had been wronged. Of how I had been betrayed. Of what I had lost. I thought at first that it would make me mad. But then — then . . ."

The gleaming eyes grew glazed. And when he spoke again, it was as if he had forgotten the visitors were with him. It was as if he was telling himself the story — a story he had told many, many times before.

"Then I saw the answer," he muttered. "I saw that light had betrayed me, but darkness would give me strength. I saw that all through my life I had been following the wrong path. I saw that evil would succeed where good had failed. And then I accepted evil. I welcomed it into my heart. And so I was reborn — as the Guardian."

Abruptly, his eyes lost their glazed look and focused on the strangers around his table. He noted the rigid and unsmiling faces, the almost untouched plates.

"Why do you not eat?" he snapped. "Do you mean to insult me?"

Lief looked through the wall nearest the table. Half hidden by mist, a mass of longing, haggard faces pressed against the glass.

"Do not mind them," smiled the Guardian, waving a casual hand at the crowd. "My subjects do not eat or drink. They are beyond such ordinary concerns of the flesh. It is your warm life they long for."

Jasmine, Barda, and Neridah stiffened even further. Lief wet his lips, shuddering inwardly as he remembered the dry, grey fingers stroking him. "Do you mean — they are the spirits of the dead?" he choked.

The Guardian seemed to bristle with indignation, and behind him the monsters stirred and growled. "Spirits of the dead?" he snorted. "Would I rule a kingdom of the dead? My subjects are very much alive, oh yes, and will be till the end of time. They waste away, they fade, but they do not age or die. They will live here, in my domain, forever. That is their reward."

"Their *reward*?" Neridah burst out. Her hands were trembling as she pushed away her plate.

The Guardian nodded, smoothing his beard thoughtfully. "A rich reward indeed, is it not?" he murmured. "Though I fear they are ungrateful. They do not appreciate their good fortune."

Lief forced himself to speak. "How did they earn their reward?" he asked.

"Ah . . ." The Guardian stretched with satisfaction. Plainly, this was the question he had been waiting for.

"The first of my subjects, the largest number, came to me in a great wind, the pride that had caused their fall still fresh within them," he murmured. "Others, like you, filled with envy and greed, have come since. To seek to win from me my most precious treasure. The symbol of my power. The great diamond, from the Belt of Deltora."

11 - The Game

Lief did not dare look at his friends, or at Neridah. He gripped the arms of his chair till his knuckles grew white, in the effort not to show what he was feeling.

But clearly the Guardian was not deceived. He smiled around the table, his red eyes greedily drinking in the expressions on the faces of his guests. Then he took the last few scraps from his plate and carelessly tossed them to the floor. The four monsters scrambled after the food, each fighting savagely for a share. He watched with a smile.

"Envy once nearly killed the greedy one at a dinner such as this," he commented idly, as the tumult at last died down. "Ah well."

Slowly, he pushed back his chair and stood up, the misshapen creatures shuffling and drooling behind him. "And now it is time for the game," he said. "The time I love the best. Come with me."

He had no need to ask them. Their feet followed him, whether they wished it or not, as he swept through one gleaming space after another, the monsters following him closely.

At last they reached a room that was plainly where he spent most of his time. Deep red curtains covered the walls, screening out the mist and the other rooms. Fine drawings and paintings, and a huge mirror in a carved frame, hung from the fabric.

On the floor was a rug rich in flowers, fruits, and birds, with a picture of a humble hermit repeated at each end. One of the Guardian's little jokes, thought Lief. Nowhere else in this valley would simple, beautiful living things be found. Upon the rug, in front of a couch heaped with cushions, stood a low table scattered with books. Hundreds more books packed shelves towering around the walls.

The Guardian did not pause, but walked straight across the room and pulled aside the curtain to reveal a glass door set into one wall. He did not open the door, but stepped aside and, with a wave of his arm, invited the companions to look through to the space beyond.

It was a small room that contained only a glass table set exactly in its center. On the table was a golden casket.

"The gem you seek is in that casket," said the

Guardian. His voice trembled. Plainly, he could hardly contain his gleeful excitement. "Whoever matches wits with me and wins can enter the room and take the prize."

Lief pressed himself against the glass of the door. The Belt of Deltora warmed faintly against his skin, proof that the Guardian spoke the truth. The great diamond was in that room. The Belt could feel it.

Barda pushed at the door with his shoulder, but it did not move.

Again the Guardian cackled. "No force can unlock this door. It is sealed by magic, and so it will remain, until you have won the right to open it. So — will you play?"

"Do we have a choice?" Jasmine muttered.

The Guardian raised his eyebrows. "Why, of course!" he exclaimed. "If you so wish, you can leave here now, empty-handed. Turn your backs on the gem you came to find. Go back where you came from! I will not stop you."

Lief, Barda, and Jasmine glanced at one another.

"If we win the game and enter the room, the diamond is ours to keep?" Lief wanted to make absolutely sure. "You will allow us to leave the valley, taking our prize with us? You swear this?"

"Certainly!" said the Guardian. "That is the rule. Your prize will be yours to keep."

"And if we fail?" Barda asked abruptly. "What then?"

The Guardian spread his hands. The fleshy leads swung free from his wrists and the monsters stirred behind him. "Then — why, then, *you* are *mine* to keep. Then you will remain here, like all the others who have chosen to match wits with me. You will become part of the Valley of the Lost. Forever."

The companions stood motionless beside the door. Outside the small room where the casket lay, despairing grey hands brushed the glass through billowing mist.

"Will you accept the challenge?" murmured the Guardian. His eyes burned like hot coals as he waited for their answer.

"We need to know more before we decide," said Barda evenly.

But Neridah was shaking her head. "*I* do not need to know more!" she exclaimed. "*I* have already decided. These three can do what they wish, but I will play no game!"

The Guardian bowed, though the corner of his mouth twitched with scorn. "Then you may go, lady," he said, carelessly waving his arm.

Neridah staggered as the spell that had bound her was broken. She backed away, then turned and ran from the room without looking back.

The Guardian sighed. "A pity," he muttered. "I thought she, of all of you, would find the diamond's lure impossible to resist. Perhaps, even now, she will change her mind and return. The smell of greed and envy is strong on her."

He turned to the creatures at his heels and petted them, one by one. "*You* sensed it keenly, did you not, my sweets?" he crooned. The monsters grunted and snuffled agreement, rubbing their bloated faces adoringly against his hands.

Without bothering to turn around, he flicked a finger in the companions' direction. With relief they felt their invisible bonds relax. Suddenly they could move freely.

The Guardian strolled to the mirror and began looking at himself with appreciation, smoothing his beard and smiling. Lief's fingers itched to reach for his sword, to attack. But he knew, as Barda and Jasmine did, that it would be no use. Hate, Greed, Pride, and Envy were facing them, jagged teeth bared. At a single warning sound the Guardian would turn and cast another spell — a spell even more powerful, perhaps, than the last.

"It is time for me to sleep," he said at last, turning away from the mirror with a yawn. "Unlike my subjects, I still have these needs of the flesh. What more do you wish to know?"

He is sure that we long for the diamond, Lief thought. He felt our need, as we looked at the casket. Still — his need is great, too. He pretends he does not care, but he dearly wants us to play his game. His pride drives him to prove himself more powerful and clever than we are, to crush and defeat us. That is his weakness.

"We cannot make up our minds to play unless we know more about the game," Jasmine said loudly. "What is it? How is it played?"

The Guardian frowned, hesitating.

"You *want* us to play, do you not?" Lief urged. "And we — we want the diamond, I confess. But we would be fools to endanger our freedom blindly. We need to know that it is *possible* to win."

The Guardian's eyes narrowed. "Of course it is possible!" he snapped. "Do you accuse me of cheating?"

"No," said Lief. "But some games are matters of chance, and luck. *Your* game may be one of these. And if so — "

"Mine is not a game of chance!" shouted the Guardian. "It is a battle of wits!"

"Then prove it," Barda said quietly. "Tell us what we must do."

The Guardian thought for a moment. Then he smiled. "It seems that you are to be worthy players," he said. "Very well. I will tell you. All you must do is find out one word. The word that will unlock the door. And that word is — my true name."

The companions stared at him in silence. Of all the things they might have expected, this was the last.

The Guardian nodded with satisfaction, well

pleased by their surprise. "The clues to the riddle are in this palace," he added teasingly. "And the first, hidden in this very room!"

Barda straightened his shoulders. "We would be grateful for some time alone to discuss our decision, sir," he said, using his most polite and formal voice.

"Certainly!" The Guardian bowed. "I am a very reasonable man, and will allow you that courtesy. But I pray you, do not try my patience. I will return in a short time, and then I must have your answer."

Gathering his creatures' leads in his hands, he turned and left them.

12 - The Search

As soon as they were alone, Jasmine ran to the glass door and stared through it once more. "There is another door in there!" she whispered. "A door that leads to the outside. See? In the corner."

"And so? What is your plan?" asked Barda warily.

Jasmine's eyes were sparkling fiercely. "It is simple. We will tell the Guardian that we will play his stupid game. Then, when he is asleep, we will find a way of breaking into this room. We can steal the gem, leave by the other door, and be out of this valley before he wakes."

"No!" Lief exclaimed impulsively.

Jasmine glanced at him in annoyance. "Are you afraid?" she demanded. "Afraid of his magic?"

Lief hesitated. It was not quite that. It was something else. That niggling memory at the corner of his mind. A warning. Something about the diamond . . .

"We would be foolish not to be afraid, Jasmine," said Barda. "The man's powers are great, and he is plainly mad. Whoever he once was, the Shadow Lord has possessed him body and soul."

He was bending over the low table, sorting quickly through the books that lay there. Lief realized that Barda, practical as ever, was checking to see if the Guardian's name, or part of it, was scribbled in the front of one of the volumes. He moved to help him.

"You will never find out his name that way!" Jasmine hissed furiously. "If it were that simple those poor souls outside the windows would have — "

Lief's gasp of surprise interrupted her. At the bottom of one of the piles of books he had seen something familiar. A small, faded blue volume. He snatched it up and opened it.

As he had half-hoped, half-feared, it was *The Belt of Deltora.* The book he had so often studied, at home in Del. The book he had last seen in the dungeon where his father lay chained and helpless.

And now it was here. Here, in the Valley of the Lost! His heart pounding, he held up the book for Barda and Jasmine to see. Barda frowned.

"That the Guardian has a copy of this book means nothing," he said. "For surely there were many copies made, not just one. They must lie in many forgotten places, all over the kingdom."

"The Guardian is a servant of the Shadow Lord — that much is certain, from what he told us," argued Lief. "And if he has been studying this book, it is because the Shadow Lord has told him to do so. The Guardian pretends to think that we are ordinary strangers, seeking the diamond out of simple greed. But perhaps he has known all along that we are not."

"Then why bother with all this talk of a game?" Jasmine muttered. "He could kill us whenever he chose!"

Lief shuddered. "Perhaps he is just entertaining himself. Playing with us, as a cat plays with a mouse."

"Perhaps," said Barda. "But perhaps not. He did not know *when* we would come. And if he has been warned of a boy, a man, and a girl with a black bird, he may not realize that we are the ones. Kree is not with us, Jasmine is dressed as a boy, and we came here with Neridah."

"At least, then, she was of some use," Jasmine sniffed.

Lief was frantically flicking through the little book. On every page were well-remembered words and phrases, but he was looking for just one thing. The passage about the powers of the diamond.

At last, he found it.

† **The diamond is the symbol of innocence, purity, and strength. Diamonds gained nobly, and with a pure heart, are a powerful force for good. They give courage and**

strength, protect from pestilence, and help the cause of true love. But take heed of this warning: Diamonds gained by treachery or violence, or desired out of envy or greed, are ill omens, and bring bad fortune. Great evil comes upon those who gain them without honor.

"This — this is what I was trying to remember," said Lief rapidly, showing the passage to his companions. "*This* is why we cannot steal the diamond!"

His friends looked at the book, then at one another. "This warning is not for us!" Jasmine protested. "Why, we do not want the gem out of greed or envy. We would be stealing it for a good reason. We would be rescuing it from the hands of evil and restoring it to its rightful place!"

Lief shook his head. "The words are clear," he insisted. "The diamond must be gained without force or trickery. Otherwise it will bring us nothing but ill — as it has brought the Guardian!"

"And so . . . ?" muttered Barda.

Lief sighed, closing the book and pushing it back into its place on the table. "The Guardian must give it to us freely. And there is only one way we can make him do that. His pride is his weakness, and this game of his is important to that pride. I believe if we can win it, he will be forced to — "

At that moment, they heard the sound of footsteps. The Guardian was returning. He swept into the room, his pets lumbering behind him.

"Well?" he demanded. "Have you made your decision?"

Lief and Barda looked quickly at Jasmine. She paused, then grimaced and gave a slight nod. Barda stepped forward.

"Yes," he said firmly. "We will play."

The monsters whined and pulled at their leads in excitement. The Guardian's eyes burned.

"Excellent!" he hissed. He pointed at a tall, unlit candle that stood on the table below the mirror. A flickering yellow flame appeared.

"The life of this candle will be the time you have to open the door into the casket room," he said. "If the door remains unopened when the candle dies, you will admit defeat and become mine. Agreed?"

"Agreed." The companions said the word together, without flinching.

The Guardian again rubbed his hands. "I wish you good night, then," he smiled. "Explore as you wish. The first clue is in this room, as I told you. In one way it is hidden. In another, it is as plain as the nose on your face."

He walked to the door, but before going on he turned once more. "A word of advice. You have one chance to open the door, and one chance only. Do not waste your chance on a guess."

He smiled thinly. "I will see you in the morning. To claim my victory."

With that, he swept from the room, with his

creatures following him. But as soon as he was out of their sight, his triumphant, cackling laughter began. It echoed around the glass walls of his palace like a hundred voices, fading slowly into the distance, as he went to his rest.

*

For an hour the companions searched the room, seeking anything, anything at all, that would give them a clue to the Guardian's name.

The books on the shelves were of no use. They crumbled to dust as Barda pulled them from their places. The papers in the drawers of the cabinets were yellowed and brittle. They, too, cracked and crumbled at a touch. The pictures revealed no clue. There was nothing behind the curtains but glass and mist.

"He thinks he has everything — but he has nothing!" exclaimed Jasmine. "His wonderful food is ashes. His beautiful books are dust. His companions are disgusting, drooling beasts. His kingdom is a place of misery. How can he be so blind?"

"It is *we* who are blind," Barda said through gritted teeth, his eyes on the slowly dripping candle. "He said there was a clue in this room, and I am sure he was telling the truth. But what clue? Where?"

"He said there was a clue *hidden* in this room!" Lief buried his face in his hands, trying to concentrate. "We have looked under everything, behind everything, inside everything. So that means it is hidden in another way."

"Hidden by magic!" Jasmine looked around the room in desperation. "And that would make sense of the other thing he said — that in one way it was hidden, and in another it was as plain as the nose on your face."

"The nose on your face! Why, of course!" thundered Barda, leaping to his feet. As his companions watched, astonished, he strode across the room and looked into the mirror. For a moment the others saw his face, strangely softened and youthful, reflected in the glass. Then the image disappeared and words appeared, shining white in the flickering light of the candle.

My secret name awaits within.
My first, the first of Pride's great sin
My second and my last begin
The sum of errors in the twin
My third begins a sparkle bright—
The treasure pure? The point of light?
My fourth, the sum of happiness
For those who try my name to guess.

"But it makes no sense!" cried Jasmine in dismay. "No sense at all!"

"It does," said Barda. "I have seen things like it before. It is a puzzle."

"The rhyme tells us how many letters are in the Guardian's name," said Lief slowly. "It tells us how to find out what the letters are. But it is more difficult by far than any puzzle I have ever solved."

He gripped the Belt of Deltora, wishing with all his heart that the topaz was at its full strength. Often before it had cleared and sharpened his mind. But its power increased as the moon grew full, and lessened as the moon waned. Tonight there was no moon at all.

If he and his companions were to solve this puzzle, they would have to solve it alone.

13 - Sparkles Bright

After copying the words from the mirror onto a scrap of paper that Jasmine found among her treasures, the companions sat and talked.

"The first line means simply that the name is to be found from clues within the palace," Lief said. "Agreed?"

"Even I can see that!" exclaimed Jasmine, as Barda nodded. "But what of all the rest?"

"The next line means that the first letter of the name we seek is the same as the first letter of Pride's great sin."

"Well, that appears simple, too," said Barda. "The first letter of Pride is P."

"But that is hardly a puzzle at all!" Jasmine objected. "Surely it cannot be so easy."

"It is not," Lief said gloomily. "Do you not see,

Barda? 'Pride' has a capital letter. It is a name. The name of one of the Guardian's pets."

"And the Guardian told us that none of his creatures had the fault for which it was named," groaned Jasmine. "Pride's sin must be envy, greed, or hatred. Ah — I begin to see now how this puzzle works. The first letter of the Guardian's name must be E, G, or H."

"But how are we to guess which one?" Barda exploded. "I do not even remember which creature was which! The Guardian is not playing fair, for all he said!"

"I am sure he is," said Lief, tapping the pencil on the paper. "The triumph he hopes to enjoy would be meaningless otherwise. Somewhere in the palace there must be another clue."

"Then we had better find it! Quickly!" exclaimed Jasmine, jumping up with a nervous glance at the candle. It was burning down alarmingly fast.

Her fear was catching. Lief felt his heart begin to pound. He forced himself to be still, and put his hand on the Belt of Deltora. His fingers found the amethyst, and as they pressed against it, his heart slowed and a soothing calm settled over him. He took a deep breath.

"We must not panic and begin rushing around without a plan," he said quietly. "Panic will stop us from thinking clearly. It is our enemy."

"Time is our enemy also, Lief," Barda reminded

him sharply. "We have been at this task hours already, and we are no further ahead."

"But we are," said Lief. "We know that the Guardian's name has five letters, because the rhyme speaks of 'my first,' 'my second,' 'my third,' 'my fourth,' and 'my last.' We know that the first letter is E, G, or H. And we know that the second and the last letters are both the same."

"How do we know that?" Jasmine was fidgeting, anxious to be away.

"The rhyme tells us so." Lief read the words aloud.

My second and my last begin
The sum of errors in the twin.

As Jasmine nodded anxiously, Lief glanced over the rest of the rhyme, and suddenly saw something else.

"And I believe — I believe I know what the fourth letter is!" he exclaimed. Again, he read aloud.

My fourth, the sum of happiness
For those who try my name to guess.

"How much happiness has come to those who have tried to guess the Guardian's name?" he asked.

"None, from what we hear," said Barda grimly.

"Exactly. And because the word 'sum' is used, I would guess that the Guardian is playing a little trick here. The fourth letter is in fact a number. Zero. Which when written down is the same as O."

As the others stared, he began scribbling under

the rhyme. When he had finished, he turned the paper so they could see what he had done.

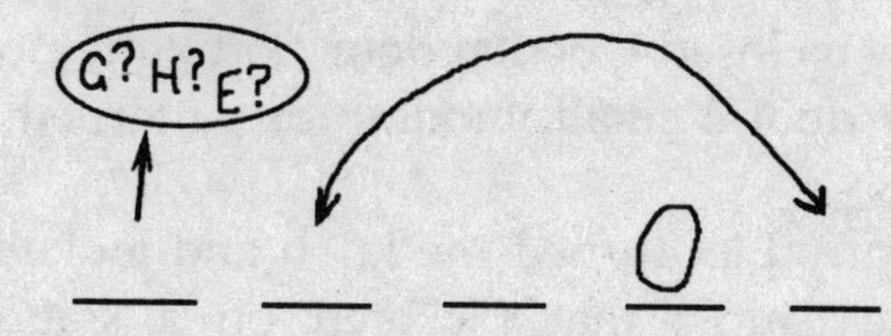

"There," Lief said. "Now we can begin filling in the blanks."

He stood up, wishing that he felt as confident as his words had sounded. "We will search the palace room by room," he said. "Wherever we go, we will look for things that match the rhyme."

Together they left the study and began the search. One room, then another, and another, yielded no clue, though they looked carefully at every piece of furniture, every rug, every ornament.

The palace was vast. They moved on and on, the lilting music following them, trying to keep calm and alert. For a while there were small sounds of movement other than their own — echoing, faraway sounds as of soft footsteps, of doors opening and closing. But at last the music stopped, and the other sounds stopped also.

Now they worked in complete silence. It was hard not to hurry. Hard not to begin rushing, skimping the search. In all their minds was a picture of the candle, dripping, dripping, relentlessly burning away.

Finally they came to a room which, like the Guardian's study, was screened by curtains and sealed by a closed wooden door. Soft light glowed behind the door's small window of patterned, colored glass.

Gently Lief turned the knob and looked in. Despite the candle that flickered on a stand beside the door, the room was dim. It took a moment for him to make out the huge pile of soft cushions in one corner.

The Guardian was lying there, asleep. But he was not alone. His four pets shared his bed, their fleshy leads tangling around them like pale snakes. And the creatures were awake. They turned their terrible heads to the door. Their teeth gleamed as they growled, long and low.

Hastily, Lief jerked backwards and closed the door again.

"We cannot go in there," he whispered. "It is his bedroom. And the creatures are with him."

"We will surely have to face them in the end," Barda whispered back. "How else will we have any hope of finding out what Pride's fault is?"

They stood, undecided, staring at the closed door. Then Jasmine's face grew puzzled. She pointed to the colored glass window. "There is something strange about this," she murmured. "I have just noticed it. Look!"

"It is certainly odd. There is a diamond or a star in every square except the last," said Barda, peering at the glass.

"Yes!" Jasmine snatched the paper from Lief's hands and read out two of the lines from the rhyme:

My third begins a sparkle bright —

The treasure pure? The point of light?

She looked up eagerly, to see if they understood. "Diamonds and stars are both bright sparkles," she said. "The rhyme is asking us which one of them should go in the last square. A diamond, which is a treasure. Or a star, which is a point of light."

"So the third letter of the Guardian's name is the beginning letter of one of those two. It is D, or S." Lief took the paper from Jasmine and made a note on his diagram, gnawing at his lip, fighting down his excitement.

They stared at the panes of colored glass till the pattern blurred in front of their eyes, but with no result.

"There is not any sense to it!" growled Barda at last. "There are sixteen squares in all. But they seem to be arranged simply according to someone's fancy."

Lief agreed. And Jasmine, now that her excitement had died, was growing more and more uneasy.

"Perhaps the mystery is connected with sixteen," Barda muttered, refusing to be beaten. "Sixteen is a useful number, for it divides easily into smaller, equal parts. The platoons at the palace numbered sixteen. Often, when we were marching in formation on the parade ground, we would begin together, then split into eights, then fours, then . . ."

His voice trailed off. His jaw had dropped. He was staring fixedly at the window. "Look!" he said huskily.

His blunt finger drew a cross through the center of the window, dividing it into four equal parts.

"The whole makes no sense," he said. "But if instead of seeing it as one large square made of sixteen smaller squares, we see four squares, each containing four smaller squares, what happens then?"

Lief looked, and it was as if he was seeing the window with new eyes. Now it was made up of four blocks. Two on the top, two on the bottom.

In the first block, there were three stars and one diamond. In the block next to that, there were two stars and two diamonds. In the third block, the one directly below the first, there was one star and three diamonds. And in the fourth block, the one that contained the blank square . . .

"One diamond is added each time," hissed Barda, his eyes alive with relief, "and one star taken away. So the last square must contain *no* stars, and — *four diamonds*!"

"Yes!" Lief could hardly believe how simple it was. But it had not seemed simple until Barda worked it out. And all because he remembered his days as a palace guard, thought Lief, writing a D above the third dash on his paper.

Barda watched with satisfaction. "Two letters filled in!" he said. "Now — shall we face the creatures?"

14 - The Name

Gently, they opened the bedroom door once more. The Guardian had not moved, but now the monsters were sprawled all over him. Hearing intruders, all of them raised their heads and snarled threateningly.

"This is impossible!" breathed Barda. "They will not let us near him. How can we find out about them from here?"

"Perhaps we can call them by name," Jasmine suggested. "Each in turn."

"Well, do not call Greed first, that is all I ask," murmured Lief.

"Why?" Jasmine asked.

Lief grew very still. He had spoken without thinking. He had blurted out the half-joking request because of something he had not realized he knew.

"Because," he said, his heart starting to pound,

"because, when we first came to the palace the Guardian told us that the envious monster and the proud one are both afraid of Greed. So Greed cannot be the envious one, or the proud one, itself. And we also know that Greed is not greedy, for none of the monsters has the fault after which it has been named. So — that means Greed must be the most dangerous one of all, the one full of hatred."

He could tell that his friends were thinking of other things the Guardian had said. Things that at the time they had not guessed were important. But which, now, suddenly seemed very important indeed.

Without a word, they backed out of the door for a second time, and closed it behind them.

"He gave us the clues, and we did not realize!" hissed Jasmine. "What else did he say?"

"He said that Envy once nearly killed the greedy one, fighting over scraps from the table," said Barda firmly.

"If Envy tried to kill the greedy one, then it is not greedy itself," said Lief. "And it is not envious, we know that . . ."

"And it is not full of hatred!" exclaimed Jasmine. "For we have already decided that Greed is that. So Envy . . . must be the one who is proud!"

They were walking away from the door, through to another room. By now they were sure that they had no need to face the monsters. They already knew enough to work the puzzle out for themselves.

"What else did the Guardian tell us?" hissed

Lief, racking his brains. "He said . . ."

"He said that Hate is not envious!" said Jasmine triumphantly. "He said it when we first saw the beasts."

"Yes!" Lief remembered. "And Hate is not full of hatred. And it is not proud, for Envy is the proud one. So — Hate must be greedy!"

"And that leaves only one fault for Pride," said Barda slowly. "Pride is envious."

Without a word, Lief wrote E on the first dash on his paper.

And now there was only one letter left to find, for the rhyme had said that the second and last letters of the name were the same. Barda repeated the clue:

My second and my last begin
The sum of errors in the twin . . .

"I have not the smallest idea what this could mean," Jasmine confessed. "I feel I am stupid, but — "

"If you are stupid, then so am I," growled Barda. "It has been a mystery to me from the start."

And Lief could not think what the strange lines could possibly mean, either. All he knew was that somewhere in this glass-walled maze was the last clue, and they had to find it.

Filled with desperate energy, they hurried from room to gleaming room, searching everywhere for some sign that would help them solve the riddle. But they found nothing. Nothing but magnificent emptiness.

Finally they turned a corner and Jasmine groaned. "But we have been here before!" she exclaimed. "We have already searched this room."

Lief and Barda looked around them and realized that Jasmine was right.

"There is nowhere left to look!" Barda's face was lined with weariness, heavy with despair.

Outside the windows, heavy mist rolled in darkness, shadowy figures drifted, fingers trailed across glass, haunted eyes stared. How much time had passed? Lief found he did not know. He clutched at the Belt under his shirt as he felt panic rising within him once more.

"The clue is here somewhere. We know it," he said, managing to keep his voice steady, the amethyst cool under his fingers. "We will simply begin the search again."

They moved on, and on, rechecking every space, till they reached the curtained study where they had begun.

"We searched this room from top to bottom," Barda muttered. "Surely there is no point . . ."

But they had to enter the study. None of them could resist the urge to look at the candle, to know how much time they had left.

Lief had braced himself for what he might see, but even he could not keep back a gasp of horror as he saw how low the flame now burned. The candle was just a stub, almost smothered by a thick mass of hardened drips. It could not last much longer.

"We cannot go on with this," Jasmine said urgently. "We must smash the glass door, take the diamond, and run, Lief, whatever you say. We must do it now!"

"She is right, Lief, I fear," said Barda, his eyes on the flame.

Lief shook his head despairingly. He knew, *knew*, that this would be a terrible mistake. Yet what choice had they? There was plainly no time to waste. No time to search the palace again. No time to think . . .

Jasmine had begun darting around the room, looking for something heavy that she could use to shatter the glass. Finding nothing better, she swept the books off the low table and began dragging it determinedly towards the door.

"No!" shouted Lief. "You must not!"

Jasmine swung around furiously. "I must! Do you not understand, Lief? What is the matter with you? It is too late now to worry about a warning in some old book! We cannot win the diamond. The Guardian's rhyme, with its riddling talk of twins that do not exist, has defeated us. This is the only way!"

She turned again and went on heaving at the table. After a brief hesitation, Barda went to join her. Pushing her aside, he lifted the table clear of the rug and carried it to the glass door.

Lief sprang at him, pulling urgently at his arm. But he had no chance against Barda's strength. The big man shook him off ruthlessly, sending him sprawling to the ground.

"Stand back," Barda said grimly. "The glass will shatter. Cover your eyes."

Lief crawled to his knees, his head spinning. Barda was already swinging the table back, steadying himself, preparing to strike. Lief ducked his head. The rug, with its flowers, fruit, and birds, was soft under his hands. The two hermits stared solemnly up at him. Two pairs of eyes. Two beards. Two long, plain robes, tied at the waist . . .

Lief stared. The blood rushed to his face. "Twins!" he shouted, staggering to his feet. "Barda, stop! The twins! I have found them!"

He pointed desperately at the rug as Barda slowly lowered the table and Jasmine stamped with frustration and anger.

"They were here all the time!" Lief babbled. "We hardly noticed them because they were under the table, and under our feet. But now you can see clearly. The hermits seem exactly alike. They look like twins! But they are not exactly alike at all!"

By this time, Jasmine and Barda were by his side, staring at the rug. Lief snatched out the paper he had stuffed in his pocket.

"The sum of errors in the twin," he read. "That must mean the number of differences between one hermit and the other."

"*Are* there differences?" demanded Jasmine, glancing worriedly over her shoulder at the weak candle flame. "Where?"

"Look at the cord around the waist," Lief urged. "In one picture it is knotted on the left side, in the other it is knotted on the right."

"And the bird!" Barda exclaimed. "In one picture it has a crest, in the other it does not."

"There are more bees coming from the hive in one than in the other," Jasmine added, drawn into the search in spite of herself. "And look — one tree has berries, the other has flowers."

"The toadstools on one side are spotted, the others are plain," Barda pointed out.

"That makes five differences," said Lief. "And there is another. One tree has a branch of leaves on the top left-hand corner, the other does not. Six differences."

"The hermit is holding three stems in one picture, and only two in the other! Seven!" whispered Jasmine.

They looked carefully, but could see nothing more.

"The number is seven," muttered Barda, his voice harsh with relief. "The letter we are looking for is S."

"No!" Jasmine was pointing again at the rug. "Wait, I see something else! The sack beside him. One sack has a tie. The other does not."

"You are right!" Lief exclaimed. "Eight! So the letter we are looking for, the second letter of the Guardian's name, and the last, is not S, but E."

"We have already had an E," hissed Jasmine.

"Ah, he is cunning," growled Barda. "He thought we would be tricked by that. And we nearly were!"

Lief scribbled on his diagram, then showed them.

"Eedoe. His name is Eedoe." Jasmine collapsed on the couch behind her. "Oh, we have done it!"

In the relieved silence that followed, Lief suddenly became aware that the soft music that had filled the air the night before had begun again. No doubt that meant that the Guardian had woken.

He glanced at the candle. The wick was flickering uncertainly, swimming in a pool of melted wax. The flame was about to go out. But that did not matter now.

The hermits on the rug looked up at him with sad eyes. No reason for sadness now, my friends, he thought. We have nearly . . .

And then he saw it.

One hermit's arm, the arm on which the bird sat, was held above the tie of his robe. The other was not.

Lief stared stupidly at the paper in his hand. His chest grew tight. He was finding it hard to breathe.

"Lief, what is the matter?" hissed Jasmine. But Lief could not answer. He walked stiffly to the glass door.

"Say it!" Barda urged. "Say, 'Eedoe'!"

Lief wet his lips. "The name is not Eedoe," he said huskily. "There are nine differences, not eight. The missing letter was N. The name — the Guardian's secret name — is — Endon."

15 - The Casket

The door swung silently open. The glass table, the golden casket, lay waiting. But Lief, Barda, and Jasmine stood where they were, gripped by horror.

"It cannot be!" Jasmine whispered. "The Guardian is too old to be King Endon! He looks as old as time!"

"He has lived as the servant of evil for sixteen years," said Lief drearily. "Evil has eaten him from within. Even Father would not recognize him now." His heart ached as he thought of what his father would feel, if he ever had to know what his friend had become.

"Jarred always said that Endon was weak," Barda growled. "Foolish and weak. Protected from the world, and used to flattery and power. But still he loved him, and tried to protect him. He saved Endon from the palace, and certain death. And for what? For this!"

"How could Father know that Tora would refuse to help?" cried Lief. "How could he know that Endon would turn to the dark side, to regain all he had lost?"

"Do not call him Endon," Barda muttered. "He is not Endon any longer, but the Guardian. And he has regained nothing! He is deceived and used. He is unloved, alone . . ."

Jasmine gasped, her eyes wide and alert. "He is alone," she repeated. "Alone! Where is the queen? Where is the heir?"

The others were silent. Their shock had for a moment driven all other thoughts from their minds. But now they saw that Jasmine had seized on the really important question.

"Father said Queen Sharn was strong," Lief said. "Strong — and brave. Not at all the spoiled, petted palace doll she appeared. Perhaps she refused to stay with Endon, once he began to listen to the Shadow Lord, once he began to become the Guardian. Perhaps she took the child, and fled."

He turned to them, his face alight with hope. "And if that is true, if Sharn and the heir are living safely somewhere else, it does not *matter* what Endon has become. The heir has always been the one we had to find."

At that moment, somewhere in the palace, he

heard footsteps and low, growling sounds. Coming closer. His skin crawled.

"Quickly!" he muttered.

He hurried into the small room, with Barda and Jasmine close behind him. Together they approached the table and stood before it.

But before Lief could lift a hand, there was a sound at the door. The Guardian was standing there, his seamed, ruined face writhing with astonishment, fury, and baffled pride. Behind him, the monsters snarled.

"So," spat the Guardian. "You discovered my name. Did it surprise you?"

"A little," said Barda evenly.

The Guardian sneered. But Lief thought he could see, deep in the red eyes, a gleam of reluctant respect.

"Only one other has ever done so," he said. "And he — he found the truth so hard to bear that he refused to enter this room and claim his prize. He left the valley, cursing me. Saying that he and his cause, whatever that may be, wanted nothing that had been tainted by my possession."

With a jolt, Lief realized who that man must have been. The man who had travelled far and wide across Deltora, seeking allies for his cause and money for arms and supplies. The man who had warned them so earnestly against coming to the Valley of the Lost. Who had always said, so bitterly, that the battle for Deltora must be fought without the king, without magic. Who had told them so firmly that their quest was pointless.

"Doom," he murmured, and felt Jasmine and Barda stiffen beside him.

The Guardian laughed mockingly. "I never knew his name, though he, at last, knew mine. It is a shame that he did not stay. There was a bitterness and hatred within him that warmed my heart, and made my creatures glad."

He stroked his beard, looking at the companions slyly. "Will you follow his example, and run?"

"No, we will not," said Barda boldly. "We will take our prize."

Lief put his hands on the golden casket. His neck burned as the Guardian's red eyes stared from the door. The Guardian. His father's friend Endon, hideously changed.

And Doom has known it all the time, he thought angrily. Yet he did not tell us. No, he kept it to himself. As he keeps everything. Trusting no one. No one but himself. Whatever the cost.

The beasts at the door whimpered and growled. Lief knew they could feel his anger. It was like meat and drink to them. This was not the time to think of things that did not matter. He pressed the catch. The lid of the casket flew up.

And inside, nestled on a bed of black velvet, a great diamond gleamed.

Lief snatched up the gem and whirled around, clutching it tightly.

"Get out!" the Guardian hissed. "Take your prize, and go!"

The door leading into the valley swung open. Mist billowed into the room, mingled with the sound of soft, sighing voices.

"Lief!" urged Barda, trying to pull Lief towards the opening.

But Lief stood his ground, feeling the blood rush into his face.

"Why do you stay?" snarled the Guardian. "Is it not enough that you have won? Must you jeer at me, too?"

"You have cheated us," Lief cried, his voice trembling with anger. He held out the jewel, gleaming on the palm of his hand. "This gem may be a diamond. But it is not the diamond from the Belt of Deltora!"

"I never promised you more than what was in the casket!" the Guardian blustered. "I said to you clearly, 'you may take your prize and go.' That is all."

"You told us your treasure was the diamond from the Belt of Deltora," Lief insisted. "And the real gem was here, when first you showed us this room. But now it has gone."

He moved a step forward, ignoring the monsters' snarls. "You moved it, Guardian, once we were safely out of the way, searching other parts of your palace," he shouted. "You replaced it with another gem. So that even if we won your game, your real treasure would not be lost."

The Guardian's eyes narrowed. "How can you know this?" he spat.

"It does not matter how I know," Lief cried. "The important thing is, you have lied and cheated. You, who make so much of following the rules."

"And did *you* follow the rules?" the Guardian jeered. "Yes! I took my jewel from the casket, and hid it outside in the mist. The gem I put in its place should more than satisfy your greed."

Panting with rage, he moved towards them, his creatures growling around his feet. "But who was watching me?" he spat. "Who stole the diamond from its hiding place, as soon as I turned my back? The fourth member of your party. The one who refused to play the game. Who pretended to have left the valley!"

"Neridah?" gasped Lief. "But . . . we knew nothing of this!"

"So you say," sneered the Guardian.

"Of course we did not know!" Jasmine was already at the doorway, almost hidden in the swirling mist. "If we had, would we have wasted our time on your stupid game? Where is she? Which way did she go?"

The Guardian shrugged. "It does not matter to you," he said. "You have your prize."

Lief stepped forward, his fists clenched. The creatures snarled.

"Lief, no!" snapped Barda. "Forget this. We must try to find Neridah's tracks. By now she will be hours away."

But Lief paid no attention. His eyes were fixed on the Guardian. "Where is Neridah?" he asked softly. "She has not left the valley, has she? You know where she is, and the diamond, too."

"And if I do know," the Guardian said, just as softly, "I will not be telling you. Did you really think I would give you the most important thing in my life? The thing that is the symbol of my lord's favor? The thing that has brought me power and riches?"

"It has brought you dust and ashes, Guardian," spat Lief. "It has surrounded you with misery. You gained it through cunning, trickery, theft, and violence. Its curse is upon you. And in your heart you know it."

Something flickered in the red eyes. "Who are you?" the Guardian murmured. "Who are you, that you know so much?"

"I have read *The Belt of Deltora,* as you have done."

"It is more than that, I think," the Guardian said. "I think you are the ones! The ones of whom I was told." He nodded to Jasmine and her hand reached up unwillingly and pulled the cap from her head. Her black hair fell, tangling, to her shoulders.

The Guardian smiled grimly. "And so I was deceived," he said. "The black bird, of course, remained outside the mist. And the fourth member of the party, the thief, was merely following you to profit by your cleverness. Ah — how nearly I let you slip through my fingers."

Once again his red eyes turned on Lief. "Give it to me," he commanded. "Give me the Belt of Deltora!"

Lief felt his hands move to his waist. His fingers found the clasp of the Belt. Sweat breaking out on his forehead, he forced them away from it, pushing them with all the force of his will over the gems that studded the medallions. His hand slid over the topaz, the ruby, the opal . . . and came to rest on the lapis lazuli, the heavenly stone, the talisman. He curled his fingers over it, and held it fast.

"That will not protect you," snarled the Guardian. He strode forward with Envy, Greed, Hate, and Pride growling and drooling around his feet. He reached out, and his hands fastened on the Belt like claws.

His eyes glowed with triumph, then suddenly widened, burning, burning like pits of fire. Staring into them, fixed in terror, Lief seemed to see a thousand pictures leaping in the flames.

But the Belt was icy cold.

The Guardian's mouth gaped in a shriek of agony. And the monsters — the monsters were capering around him, throwing up their heads and howling, straining at their leads, trying to get away from him.

Lief staggered. He was released. The spell was broken. The Guardian fell to his knees, throwing back his head, still clinging to the Belt as though he could not let go. Envy, Greed, Hate, and Pride turned on him in a frenzy, their jaws frothing, their terrible teeth ripping and tearing at him, shredding his robe to ribbons, slicing into the shrivelled grey flesh beneath.

And then, with a thrill of horror, Lief saw what the robe had hidden. Saw the four great, oozing lumps on the Guardian's chest. Saw the pulsing, fleshy cords that arose from them, twisting and snaking through his sleeves and on to the swollen necks of the savage, attacking beasts. The Guardian had called Hate, Greed, Envy, and Pride his pets, but they were part of him. Vile growths from his own body.

"Release me!" screamed the Guardian. "They are eating me alive! Cut the cords! Oh, I beg you!"

Lief's sword was in his hand. Shuddering, his ears ringing with the shrieks of the man and the roars of the beasts, with his companions' shouts of horror, he swung at the lashing ropes of flesh, slicing them through.

Yellow-green liquid gushed from the wounds. The cords writhed, their cut ends flopping horribly to the ground. The monsters swayed, then fell. For an instant they lay twitching. Then they were still.

The Guardian's fingers loosened. His withering face turned up to Lief's. In the red eyes, the fires were dying.

"The diamond," he croaked. "Take it! It is with her. Where she lies. The stream . . ."

He crumpled and fell backward. Lief, Jasmine, and Barda turned and ran.

16 - Answers

Neridah lay face up in the stream, the slow water drifting over her unseeing eyes, her hair billowing over the rock on which she had hit her head. In the open palm of her cold, cold hand lay a great diamond.

"It seems that the Guardian did not kill her," Jasmine murmured, wondering. "It was just ill fortune that she tripped while she was crossing the stream. Ill fortune that she hit her head and drowned."

Realizing what she had said, she glanced at Lief and bit her lip. "I am sorry," she muttered. "If I had had my way, no doubt we would be lying here, or somewhere like it, ourselves. The curse — is strong."

"Strong enough for the Guardian to know that he did not have to fear theft," Barda said grimly. "The diamond could be relied upon to act before the thief escaped the valley."

"Take care!" cried Jasmine, as Lief reached into the water.

But Lief shook his head. "We have nothing to fear," he said. The Belt grew hot at his waist as he lifted the great gem, dripping, from the water.

Mist swirled about him, filled with shadows, filled with whispers, as he took off the Belt and laid it on the ground. The six gems glowed on their steel medallions. The last medallion waited to be filled.

Lief pressed the great diamond down. With a tiny click, it slid into place. Into the place where it belonged. The Belt was complete.

There was a moment's breathless silence. Then the whispering began again. Louder now. Louder. The mist billowed, clumping into columns and spirals, rising from the ground and writhing upward through the trees, as though it was alive. And as it rose, figures were left blinking in the clear air. Men, women, and children looked in bewildered joy at their warming hands, at their slowly coloring robes, and at each other.

Then there was a great crack, a shattering, like the sound of breaking glass. In an instant, the valley was flooded with color and blinding light.

And when Lief, Barda, and Jasmine looked again there were people by the hundreds, by the thousands, rejoicing among the trees, under the blue sky. They were no longer grey, drifting, hollow-faced, but rich with color, warmth, and life.

Most were tall and slender, with long, smooth faces, their dark eyes shining beneath slanting eyebrows. Black, silky hair hung down their backs, the deep sleeves of their robes swept the ground. Staring at them in wonder, hardly able to accept the evidence of his own eyes, Lief remembered the Guardian's words.

The first of my subjects, the largest number, came to me in a great wind, the pride that had caused their fall still fresh within them . . .

And then he knew. These were the lost people of Tora.

⁕

The companions walked through the crowd, and everywhere hands were held out to them. But now the hands were open, filled with life and thanks.

The people of Tora had wandered in the Valley of the Lost for as long as Lief had been alive, yet they had not grown old, or changed. Old, middle-aged, and young, they remained just as they had been that day when they broke their vow. Lief, Barda, and Jasmine moved among them, hearing over and over the story of their fall.

The magic of the tunnel had protected Tora from evil for so long that the Torans had come to think they had grown perfect, as their city was perfect, and that any decision they made would be the right one. When the message from Endon came, they considered it as they considered everything: without passion, without hate, without anger. But also without warmth, without love, without pity.

"The decision did not seem a betrayal of trust," murmured a young man who held the hand of a small child. "It seemed sensible, and just. For to us, the king was a stranger. Even the Torans who went to Del with Adin, and those who went afterwards, had long ago become part of the Del palace life. They had ceased to be a bridge between our cities."

"But in our pride we forgot the magic on which our power was based," sighed an old woman, tall and straight in her scarlet robe. "The ancient vow, with the curse it embraced, was still as strong as it ever was. We did not count on that, for we looked forward, but never backward in those days. We have learned better since."

The companions walked back through the trees to the palace clearing, the crowd following silently. As they approached the clearing Lief was haunted by the feeling that he was dreaming. At any moment he might wake. At any moment he might see the palace, gleaming like a jewel, and the Guardian, red eyes staring, beckoning through swirling mist.

But the palace had gone, as if it had never been. In its place was a small wooden hut. Flowers and wild grass grew around it, and standing at its door was a bearded man wearing a coarse gown, tied at the waist with a knotted cord. His sad eyes met Lief's. They were very familiar.

Perched on his arm was a black bird. Sitting on his hand was a small, grey bundle of fur.

Before Lief could say a word, Jasmine was running forward with a cry of joy. Then Kree was flying towards her, and Filli was leaping, chattering, to meet her. They had come down from the cliff edge the moment the mist had lifted. They had waited with their new friend patiently. But now that they saw Jasmine, they would not wait a moment longer.

*

Together once again, the companions moved to the stranger's side.

"You are the hermit — the hermit in the pictures on the rug," Lief said.

The man nodded.

"And you are the Guardian."

The man put his hand to his chest, close to his heart, as if feeling a tender place. "No longer. Thanks to you," he said quietly.

"But — you are not Endon, are you?" Lief already knew the answer, but he wanted to hear it aloud.

The man smiled. "No, I am not. My name is Fardeep. Once I was a rich man, it is true. A respected man, and very well content. But I was no king. Just the keeper of an inn in a place called Rithmere, far from here. Bandits invaded the town. My family was killed, and my inn was taken from me. The Shadow Lord, it seems, had a use for it."

The companions exchanged glances. "Could you be speaking of the Champion Inn?" Barda asked.

"You know it?" said Fardeep. "Yes. The Champion Inn was once mine. I have always liked games."

His mouth twisted ruefully as the companions shuddered. "Now the games played at Rithmere are of a different sort, I hear," he said. "And the inn is much larger, and run upon very different lines from those in my time, and for a different reason."

He sighed deeply. "But in those days the Shadow Lord's plans were not known to me. It all happened long before he took possession of Deltora. Before Endon ever became king. I knew nothing, and cared nothing, for what was ahead. I escaped Rithmere and fled to this valley seeking refuge, and peace."

He bowed his head. "But peace was denied to me. My misery and anger was felt, and used, by the one who knows how to use them best. At first I did not know he was the one who had caused my trouble. Later, as gifts were showered upon me, it did not seem to matter. I told you how it was. Pride, envy, hatred, and greed grew in me. And as time went on I became — what you saw."

Again his hand crept to his heart.

"But why did your game — the Guardian's

game — make us think your name was Endon?" Jasmine asked. "Why did that name open the door?"

"The Shadow Lord wished it," said Fardeep simply. "From the first, he wanted anyone who came here for the diamond to be deceived. To think that King Endon had turned to the dark side, and become his servant. As the Guardian, I found the idea — amusing. And as I told you, I have always liked games. That part of me had not changed."

He looked up, grim-faced. "Until you came, only the scar-faced man — Doom — had ever solved the puzzle. And the effect on him was everything my master could have hoped."

He glanced across to where the Torans had gathered, murmuring to one another. He straightened his shoulders and went to speak with them.

"We have learned one important thing from this," said Jasmine, as soon as they were alone. "It means that the Shadow Lord does not know that it is Endon's heir, not Endon himself, who is important."

"Or if he does, he does not know that we are aware of it, too," Lief answered thoughtfully.

Fardeep and the people were coming towards them. "We hope that you will stay with us, for rest while you can," Fardeep said rather stiffly, stepping forward. "We can offer you little luxury. But there is wild food enough for all now, in the valley. And friendship in abundance."

"That is luxury enough," smiled Barda. "And we will be glad to stay — for a time. We must bury our companion, Neridah. And we have much to talk about."

Fardeep's whole body relaxed in a shuddering sigh of relief. "I would not have blamed you if you had loathed the very thought," he said. He glanced over his shoulder at the crowd. "They, too, have forgiven me," he said in a low voice. "It is more than I expected. And far more than I deserve."

"We forgive you heartily," called a stout, blue-clad woman at the front of the crowd. "Your fault was only blindness, as was ours. And we will stay here, for as long as you allow it, and be grateful. For we have nowhere else to go."

"Tora is perfect, as it always was," called Barda. "It is waiting for you!"

But the people shook their heads regretfully. "We can never go back," the blue-clad woman murmured. "The stone that is the city's heart is cracked, and its fire is no more. The vow was broken, and that evil can never be undone."

It can, Lief thought. It *can* be undone.

He thought he knew how. But it was not time yet. The heir to Deltora still had to be found.

But where? Where in all the wide kingdom was the hiding place that had kept Endon, Sharn, and their child safe for so long? How could he and his companions find it, with no idea of where to look, or where to start?

For a moment he felt a sinking in his heart. Then, again he touched the Belt, heavy around his waist.

We will find the hiding place, he told himself. *Wherever it is, no matter how far. For we are not without guidance any longer. The Belt is complete. And it will show us the way.*